Cast of Characters

Kate Rebel: Matriarch of the Rebel family.

Falcon: The eldest son—the strong one. Reunited with his wife, Leah, and proud father of Eden and John.

Egan: The loner. Married to Rachel Hollister, daughter of the man who put him in jail.

Quincy: The peacemaker. Married to Jenny Walker, his childhood best friend.

Elias: The fighter. Falls in love with the daughter of his family's archenemy.

Paxton: The lover. Never met a woman he couldn't have, but the woman he wants doesn't want him.

Jude: The serious, responsible one. Back together with his first love, Paige Wheeler, and raising their son, Zane.

Phoenix: The youngest Rebel challenges his own family when he falls in love with the enemy—Rosemary McCray.

Abraham (Abe) Rebel: Paternal grandfather.

Jericho Johnson: Egan's friend from prison.

Dear Reader,

Texas Rebels: Paxton is the sixth book in the Texas Rebels series. The series is about seven brothers who deal with their father's death in different ways.

I apologize for the delay of Paxton's story. Life got in the way of finishing this book. In the spring I had to have unexpected neck surgery and there were complications that required a long hospital stay. I am now back to writing and so happy to have finally finished this book. Thank you for your patience and support!

There are two Canada geese, Henry and Henny, in this story. My husband and I live on a lake in Central Texas and these geese live in our backyard. A bobcat stalks them at night, and he finally got Henny and broke her wing. I wondered when the geese flew away in the winter if Henry would leave his Henny behind. I wanted to see if it was true they mate for life. I watched and watched and was delighted when he stayed. He never leaves her except to fly around the lake in the early morning. A true love story, as is Paxton and Remi's.

If you've read the other Rebels books, you know Paxton is accustomed to getting any beautiful woman he wants. Ironically, he falls for a woman who's not ready to get involved with anyone. It took a few sleepless nights to pull these two characters together. But like the Canada geese, they'll find a special love that will keep them together forever.

Until the next Rebel book, with love and thanks,

Linda

PS: You can email me at Lw1508@aol.com; send me a message on Facebook.com/lindawarrenauthor or on Twitter, @texauthor; write me at PO Box 5182, Bryan, TX 77805; or visit my website at lindawarren.net. Your mail and thoughts are deeply appreciated.

TEXAS REBELS: PAXTON

LINDA WARREN

⬥HARLEQUIN®WESTERN ROMANCE

Recycling programs
for this product may
not exist in your area.

ISBN-13: 978-0-373-75769-5

Texas Rebels: Paxton

Copyright © 2017 by Linda Warren

This edition published by arrangement with Harlequin Books S.A.

For questions and comments about the quality of this book, please contact us at CustomerService@Harlequin.com.

Printed in U.S.A.

www.Harlequin.com

A two-time RITA® Award–nominated author, **Linda Warren** has written forty books for Harlequin and has received the Readers' Choice Award, the Holt Medallion, the Booksellers' Best Award, the Book Buyers Best Award, the Golden Quill and the RT Reviewers' Choice Best Book Award. A native Texan, she is a member of Romance Writers of America and the West Houston chapter. She lives in College Station with her husband and a menagerie of animals, including a Canada goose named Broken Wing. You can learn more about Linda and her books at lindawarren.net.

Books by Linda Warren

Harlequin Western Romance

Texas Rebels

Texas Rebels: Egan
Texas Rebels: Falcon
Texas Rebels: Quincy
Texas Rebels: Jude
Texas Rebels: Phoenix

Harlequin American Romance

The Cowboy's Return
Once a Cowboy
Texas Heir
The Sheriff of Horseshoe, Texas
Her Christmas Hero
Tomas: Cowboy Homecoming
One Night in Texas
A Texas Holiday Miracle

Visit the Author Profile page
at Harlequin.com for more titles.

Acknowledgments

A special thanks to the ladies who spoke
with me about adoptions in Texas.

To Betty Moon for sharing her great-grandson's
heart surgery and adoption.

To Carrol Abendroth, barrel racer, for giving
me a glimpse into the rodeo scene.

And to the PRCA and the WNFR for
all their information.

All errors are strictly mine.

Dedication

To my husband, my hero, my Sonny,
for keeping me sane this past year.

Prologue

My name is Kate Rebel. I married John Rebel when I was eighteen years old and then bore him seven sons. We worked the family ranch, which John later inherited. We put everything we had into buying more land so our sons would have a legacy. We didn't have much, but we had love.

The McCray Ranch borders Rebel Ranch on the east and the McCrays have forever been a thorn in my family's side. They've cut our fences, dammed up creeks to limit our water supply, and shot one of our prize bulls. Ezra McCray threatened to shoot our sons if he caught them jumping his fences again. We tried to keep our boys away, but they are boys—young and wild.

One day Jude and Phoenix, two of our youngest, were out riding together. When John heard shots, he immediately went to find his boys. They lay on the ground, blood oozing from their heads. Ezra McCray was astride a horse twenty yards away with a rifle in his hand. John drew his gun and fired, killing Ezra instantly. Both boys survived with only minor wounds. Since my husband was protecting his children, he didn't spend even one night in jail. This escalated the feud that still goes on today.

The man I knew as my husband died that day. He couldn't live with what he'd done, and started to drink heavily. I had to take over the ranch and the raising of our boys. John died ten years later. We've all been affected by the tragedy, especially my sons.

They are grown men now and deal in different ways with the pain of losing their father. One day I pray my boys will be able to put this behind them and live healthy, normal lives with women who will love them the way I loved their father.

Chapter One

Paxton: the fifth son—the ladies' man
The cowboy's redemption.

Mother Nature spit out a nasty spray of morning mist along the beach in Port Aransas, Texas. The cool lick of water against Paxton Rebel's cheeks felt like the touch of a Popsicle. He huddled deeper in his National Finals Rodeo jacket and kept walking.

His cowboy boots made imprints in the wet sand, but the incoming tide would soon wash them away. Nothing in life stayed the same. And today the winds of change blew through his mind with a warning: if you don't change your ways, it will be the death of you. His head throbbed, his body ached and exhaustion pulled at him as if he was a man twice his age. He was too young to feel this old and worn-out.

But then December had been a month of partying and drinking and celebrating. He and his brother Phoenix had competed in the National Finals Rodeo in Vegas the first ten days in December. Phoenix had won the title in bull riding and Paxton had come in second. Losing to his brother wasn't a big deal because Phoenix deserved it.

Phoenix had become a father and married the love of his life in Vegas. He was at the beginning of something new. Although he was happy for his brother, he was feeling adrift without his partner. A part of him would miss working together on the rodeo circuit.

He and his brother Elias had continued to party in Vegas and had flown home later with gigantic headaches. They'd helped Phoenix clear some land to build a new home for his family and then there was Christmas with the whole Rebel clan. Paxton and Elias, the remaining bachelors in the family, had partied the New Year in. Waking up in his truck at Rowdy's Beer Joint, having no idea how the night had ended, was the last straw for Paxton. He knew change had to happen for him.

He'd taken a couple days off from work on the ranch to clear his head and decide his future. Even though it wouldn't be the same without Phoenix, he planned to ride the circuit another year.

The cold north wind tugged at him and he shoved his hands into the pockets of his jacket. In early January, Port Aransas was almost deserted, but peace and quiet was what he needed to help him make decisions that would affect the rest of his life.

Port Aransas had happy memories. That was why he'd chosen the place to think. When he was a kid, his brothers and parents used to come here for a vacation. Today the scenery was much different with hotels, motels and restaurants that hadn't been there years ago.

He and his brothers used to race down the beach. Phoenix was barely three, but he always tried to keep up. "Paxton, watch out for Phoenix!" his mother would shout after them. And it seemed like he'd been doing that most of his life. But in reality Phoenix had been looking out for Paxton, pulling him out of bars when things got heated, making sure he stayed off beer on rodeo days and steering him away from girls who could ruin his career. He and Phoenix had always been a team but…

The temperature had been in the sixties earlier, but now the mercury was dropping as a cold front made its way across the Gulf Coast. His cell buzzed and he pulled it out of his pocket. Heather? Who was Heather? He read the text: I'm in Killeen. Wanna hook up? He couldn't remember any Heather. It probably was a girl he had met over the holidays.

He groaned inwardly, not liking that he couldn't remember. Girls were another problem. They called him "The Heartthrob" on the rodeo circuit. He hated the nickname, but it had stuck. Even the announcers called him that. And he'd gotten into more than one fight when his friends had ragged him about it.

Girls were easy for him, though. They hung around after rodeos and invited him out. They were persistent, but now he planned to be more selective. He would have to cross that line from a wild teenager into adulthood. It was past time. He'd left his twenties behind and now he had to grow up. It might be the hardest thing he ever had to do.

His cell buzzed again and he looked at the caller ID. *Lisa.* That name he knew. His ex-fiancée. She'd been calling ever since Vegas but he hadn't picked up. For a brief moment in time he'd thought he was in love with her. He soon had learned she wasn't the woman for him, so he couldn't understand why she was calling him now. And he wasn't interested in finding out why.

He'd ended his long-time relationship with his high

school sweetheart because of Lisa. It was such a messy time with so many hurt feelings. But ultimately, breaking up with Jenny had been a good decision because he'd realized he wasn't really in love with her. They were just good friends. She'd married his brother Quincy and the two of them were happy and expecting their first child in March. Paxton felt no jealousy or animosity toward them. He had to find his own way now. And it wasn't in partying or flashy women.

Five of his brothers were married and happy. That left him and Elias searching for something they might never find.

The waves lapped at the sandy shore near his boots and gray clouds hung low on the horizon. It was time to head home. Two days on the coast in winter was enough. He stopped short when he noticed a woman in a hooded blue jogging suit struggling to get to her feet. A yellow Lab stood beside her, as if trying to help. She continued to push in the sand with her right foot and hand to no avail. He rushed forward.

She saw him approach and sank back on the damp sand. "I'm fine," she said in a raspy voice, a sign she was out of breath.

"You—"

"I'm fine. Really." This time her voice had a note of anger, and he stepped away, knowing he was invading her privacy and it was upsetting her. Against everything he'd been taught as a kid by his parents, he walked on. Even though he knew the woman needed help, he wasn't going to push it. But then some things you just don't outgrow. He looked back and she was continuing to try to stand, holding on to the Lab as if to give her a boost.

He hurried back and held out his arm, almost in her

face, and stared at her, just daring her to resist. To his amazement, she didn't. She grabbed his forearm and pulled herself up. No thank-you. No nothing. She didn't even look at him.

In the brief moment she had glanced at him earlier he'd noticed her eyes—sea green, the color of the water behind him. Warm. Inviting. Tempting. And angry. Light brown hair peeked out from the hood of her jacket and her skin was pale. Very pale, as if she'd been ill. What was she doing on the beach alone in January? She had that fragile look about her and the jogging suit hung on her thin body.

She turned, the dog at her side, her hand on its collar, and slowly made her way to the hotel behind him. Paxton shook his head. He'd never had an encounter with a woman quite like that. But it was none of his business. He just hoped that there was someone waiting for her in the hotel.

His hand unconsciously went to the spot on his arm where she'd touched him. Even through his jacket and a shirt he could still feel it. She was trembling and trying to hide it as best as she could. What stood out even more was the fact she was scared to death.

REMI ROBERTS SLOWLY made it to her room and eased onto the bed. Tears trickled from her eyes and she fought hard to control her emotions. Sadie, her dog, jumped up beside her and she wrapped her arms around the warm and solid dog to steady herself. How could she have been so stupid?

Her mother and stepfather had said she didn't need to go anywhere alone, but had she listened? Of course not. She wanted to be independent again and she wanted to prove that to her family.

She had spent so much time in therapy. She knew she was better and each day she'd grown stronger. Just not strong enough to get up from the ground. She'd adventured outside early to watch the sunrise and then had decided to just sit and watch the morning as it opened like a curtain on a play. What would this day hold? She hadn't considered how long she'd been sitting on the ground. She'd had so much confidence she could get to her feet. But she hadn't been able to. She'd tried and tried and still her stubborn left leg would not work. The accident would always be with her and she was fighting every day to get back some of her life.

As she'd struggled to stand, she'd prayed a prince charming would rescue her. Then she'd looked up and seen him. Her heart had jackknifed into her throat. He had to be the most gorgeous man she'd ever seen. A lethal grin had tugged at the corners of his perfectly shaped mouth. Beneath the cowboy hat, she'd glimpsed dark hair. His eyes were a rich caramel brown that held a sleepy-eyed allure. His face had to have been chiseled by the hand of God and stroked by the wings of angels. It was perfect. Masculine. Sexy. And sparked a raw earthiness that stirred an awakening in her lower belly.

He was a cowboy.

A lot of girls liked cowboys.

She hadn't been one of them. And today she wondered why.

She didn't know what had made her so stiff and unfriendly, but accepting his help meant she wasn't better. She still needed more therapy, more support from her family. Her life was on hold. And that meant she would lose Annie.

She couldn't lose Annie.

ON THURSDAY MORNING Paxton sat with his brothers in the Rebel Ranch office discussing the day's work. Falcon, his oldest brother, and their mom sat at their desks and the others gathered around, waiting for orders for the day. Even Grandpa was there.

"Leah and John have doctors' appointments in Houston today and I've taken the day off," Falcon said. Leah, Falcon's wife, had had a brain tumor when John was born. He was a preemie but no one would guess that today by the rowdy little boy he was. "Justin is sick so Egan is at home taking care of him because Rachel went back to teaching. Phoenix is working on his house. And Jude is helping Phoenix."

"Quincy is out for the day, too," his mother said. "Jenny has been put on bed rest and he wants to make sure she's following rules."

"Guess who that leaves to handle the feeding." Elias straightened his hat with a strong hand. "Let's go, Jericho." Elias glanced at Paxton. "Are you working?"

His mother raised her head. "I have something else for Paxton this morning, but he'll join you later."

"Sure." Elias slapped Paxton on the shoulder.

Grandpa got to his feet. "I'll help you boys. I can still ride a horse."

"We're feeding cows, Grandpa," Elias said.

"You don't think I've ever fed cows?"

They were arguing as they went out the door. Falcon followed and that left him and his mother. He knew what was coming. Something in the house needed fixing. He was good at plumbing, wiring, all kinds of contracting work. And he hated it. But sometimes he did what he had to.

He leaned forward in his chair, his hands clasped between his legs. "So what do you need?"

His mother waved a hand. "Oh, no, it's nothing like that. You know Miss Bertie Snipes?"

"Everybody knows Miss Bertie and steers clear of her. She's loony as a bat."

"Now, son, I raised you not to be judgmental or critical. Her son was killed in the marines, her only son, and it changed her. Yes, she's a little different, and she needs our help."

That rolled around in his head for a minute, and if it sounded like he thought it did, he was ready to run. "What are you talking about?"

"Quincy usually helps her with her cows since Edgar died, but he's busy this morning and I thought you would be nice enough to haul her calves to the auction barn in Cameron. If you take the shortcut, it shouldn't take you long."

Paxton jumped to his feet. "Oh, no, no!"

His mother took off her glasses and laid them on the desk alongside a picture of his dad and her when they'd first gotten married. His eyes rested on the photo and he couldn't seem to look away from all the love and the pain that was echoed there and in his heart.

"I don't want to force you to do anything. So if that's the way you feel, I'll haul the calves."

His mother was a master at playing the guilt card and it was working, like always, making him feel guilty, selfish and self-centered. A bell, like a church bell, sounded in his head. He wanted to change his life and this was where he started. By helping others. But why did it have to be a crazy old lady?

THIRTY MINUTES LATER he crossed the main highway from Rebel Road to County Road 461. Miss Bertie lived in a small white frame house with black shutters and a chain-link fence. The property was neat and clean and shaded with big oak trees. An Australian blue healer raced around the chain-link fence at the rattle of the cow trailer.

Paxton drove to the back and saw the corral was to the left. A 1990 Chevy truck was parked near the barn and a small SUV was in front of the house. He knew the SUV wasn't Miss Bertie's so she must have company. That was good. He could get this over with quickly.

Calves milled around in the corral. That was another good thing. Loading would be easy. He backed up to the wood chute and got out. Miss Bertie hurried from the house with the dog at her heels. A floppy straw hat crowned her head, and she wore a big flannel shirt and baggy jeans stuffed into work boots. In her hand was a shotgun—an old double-barrel. That gave him pause.

"Who are you coming onto my property?" She fired the words at him like bullets.

Guess his mother didn't call her.

He tipped his hat, refusing to be intimidated by the fire in her eyes. And the shotgun. "I'm Paxton Rebel. My mother sent me over to haul your calves to the auction."

"My, my." She placed the butt of the gun on the ground and leaned on the barrel, peering at him a little closer through thick glasses. "You're one of the younger ones, the bull rider who spends most of his life on the road."

"Yes, ma'am."

"Now aren't you a handsome devil?"

"I've never thought about it."

"Sure." She slapped a hand on her jean-clad thigh. "It's kind of hard to think with girls trailing behind you." She glanced toward the corral and her demeanor changed instantly. "We don't have time for small talk. Time to get these calves loaded." She inspected the trailer backed up to the loading chute. "You did that perfectly. Can tell you're a cowboy."

Paxton noticed the platform from the corral to the trailer was missing and there was no way for the calves to get into the trailer, except if they knew how to fly. "Ma'am, the ramp is missing from the corral."

She grunted. "It fell apart years ago. There's always a way. Haven't you learned that by now?" She opened the gate and walked into the pen, hollering and shouting until the calves scurried into the chute. They stopped at the trailer.

The dog barked.

"Shut up, Memphis," she scolded.

Memphis.

Paxton jumped over the fence. It was wobbly. The whole corral looked as if it was going to fall down at any minute. "This is what I was telling you. If—"

She raised the shotgun and fired into the air. Stunned for a second, he was speechless, and then he grabbed it from her hand before she could fire it again.

Yanking the gun from his hand, she said, "Don't ever take my gun."

He swallowed hard at the rough words, but he didn't falter.

"See." She pointed to the calves that were jumping into the trailer, scared for their lives. "That's how you get 'em inside. Pull your truck up and I'll close the gate."

"Crazy old woman," Paxton muttered to himself as he jumped over the fence and then pulled his truck forward. Before he could reach the back of the trailer, Miss Bertie had it already closed. But he double-checked it.

"I'll be on my way," he said more to himself than to her.

"Now wait just a minute." She pulled a piece of paper out of her shirt pocket. "There's four black with white faces, five red with white faces and two scrubby-looking things. That's eleven."

"Yes, ma'am." Did she think he would try to cheat her?

"Gotta watch those people at the auction barn. They'll cheat you if they can. Keep your eyes open."

Holy crap. "Yes, ma'am."

She pulled some money out of her pocket and handed it to him. It was a five-dollar bill. "Take this for gas."

Was she freaking kidding? Five dollars for a diesel truck wouldn't get them out of the driveway. But he knew better than not to take it.

"I'll be on my way."

She glanced toward the house and then back at him. "Just a minute. I need a favor. A big favor."

Oh, no. But what did he say?

"I don't have much time, Miss Bertie. I have to get back to the ranch to work."

"Ah, don't give me that." She grunted again. "It'll only take a few minutes."

"Well…" He felt like a fish on a hook and he knew he wasn't getting out of here without doing what she wanted. He just had a feeling it was going to be something he didn't want to do.

"When you bring my sales receipt back, I'll invite you into the house and I want you to meet my granddaughter."

Oh, crap. She was playing matchmaker. The one thing he hated most in the world.

"She's been feeling a little down lately and a nice-looking man like you could cheer her up real fast."

"Miss Bertie…"

But the old woman wasn't listening. "I'll introduce you and you can say something like what a beautiful granddaughter I have. That's it. Just a compliment to cheer her up. You can do that, can't you, Handsome?"

"I'd rather not." He figured honesty was the best place to start.

The butt of the shotgun rested on the ground. She lifted it into her hand. "I'd rather that you did. Do you know what I mean?"

No, he didn't.

"Miss Bertie, I know you're trying to help your granddaughter, but complimenting her is going to sound fake. It's not done like that these days."

"How's it done, then?"

"With a look. It's the way a guy looks at a girl or the way a girl looks at a guy to let them know they're interested. That's how it's done. You can compliment someone, but they'll probably laugh in your face."

She shrugged. "Who knows how you young folks live these days. You just come into my kitchen and give her the look, and you better do it because if you don't, I'll come looking for you. Get my drift?"

"Yes, ma'am." He climbed into his truck. "It's been a pleasure meeting you."

He sincerely hoped this would be their last meeting because he had no intention of returning to compliment her granddaughter. His mother could bring the sales receipt and he'd stay as far away as possible.

Chapter Two

One hour and thirty minutes later Paxton zoomed toward Horseshoe, Texas, and Rebel Ranch. He wasn't being manipulated by Miss Bertie. But then the seeds of guilt began to play with his mind. His dad had always said once you start a job, you make sure you finish it. He could remember when he was a kid, he and his dad were fixing a fence and it began to drizzle and then it started to sleet. But his dad worked on, saying a man always finishes the job he starts.

If he gave the sales slip to his mother, so Miss Bertie could pick up her check, that meant he hadn't finished the job. Disappointment would be in his mother's eyes and in that moment he knew he couldn't just run away like a little boy. What would it hurt to compliment Miss Bertie's plain-Jane granddaughter? He'd flirted with more girls than he could remember. One more was a piece of cake.

He turned off the highway onto County Road 461 and drove across the cattle guard, the trailer clanging. The dog raced along the chain-link fence, barking his head off. Paxton stopped the truck at the back of the house and slammed the gearshift into Park. He picked up Miss Bertie's sales receipt, which had a tag number and a description of each calf, from the console and headed for the back door.

Memphis jumped up and down, barking and wagging his tail, eager to see a person. He had a heck of a time keeping the dog from darting out the gate. A long porch adorned the back of the house with a couple of old rocking chairs. He went up the steps and knocked on the built-in-screen glass door.

"Come on in!" Miss Bertie shouted.

He opened the door and stepped into 1960, or the late 1950s. The floor was yellow-and-white linoleum and the chairs and table were an old Formica set. It reminded him of his grandmother's old house. Miss Bertie came into the kitchen and this time she wasn't wearing a hat. Her short gray hair stuck out in all directions. He wondered if she had a brush or a comb.

She winked at him. "Sweetie, come here. We have company."

"Gran, I'm riding my bike."

"We still greet company in my house. Get your butt in here."

Paxton removed his hat, ready to get this over with as fast as he could.

A girl appeared in the doorway in jogging pants and a sweatshirt with the University of Houston on it. She was thin and frail, and her clothes hung on her. Her short light brown hair framed a pretty face. Familiar sea-green eyes stared at him.

The girl from Port Aransas.

She was as stunned as he was, grabbing the door frame for support.

"Remi, sweetie, this is Paxton Rebel. And this is my granddaughter—"

"What are you doing letting a Rebel into your house?" The girl turned on her grandmother.

Miss Bertie shrugged. "I have nothing against the Rebels."

"John Rebel killed my father. Have you forgotten that?"

Oh, crap. It dawned on Paxton for the first time. This had to be Ezra McCray's daughter. He'd been younger then and had forgotten a lot of the details. But Miss Bertie's daughter, Ava, had married Ezra McCray. Paxton knew they had a son, Ruger, but he had no idea they had a daughter.

"Okay, missy, I'm not standing here and letting you paint your father as a saint. He was an evil man and I would have killed him myself, but your grandfather always stopped me. He beat your mother so many times and I begged her to leave, but she was scared to death of him. Everyone in this town was scared of him. And in case you've forgotten he tried to kill two of the Rebel boys."

"I'd rather not talk about this and I'd rather not talk to him." She nodded toward Paxton.

"Do you know what he's doing here?" Miss Bertie asked.

"No."

"He hauled my calves to the auction barn because Ruger wouldn't. Your brother is under Ira McCray's thumb and he won't let him do anything for me. These are the people you're protecting. People you don't even know. You were less than two years old when your mother took you to Houston. Later, your mother remarried and Nathan adopted you. Nathan is your father and Ezra is nothing to you."

"Gran—"

Paxton had had enough. He wasn't stepping into this land mine. He handed Miss Bertie the papers. "You can pick up your check tomorrow afternoon." He tipped his hat. "It's been a pleasure."

"Wait a minute. I want to look at this," Miss Bertie called, and he forced himself to stop and turn around. "I have to find my glasses." She disappeared down a hallway.

Remi stepped farther into the room. "What are you doing here?"

"Your grandmother just told you. I hauled her calves to the auction."

"There was no need."

"Oh, and who was going to do it? You?"

"I could have."

"I don't think so. You have a hard time standing and you're pale and thin." The moment the words left his mouth he knew they were not something you'd say to a woman. And he was right. Her sea-green eyes simmered with anger.

She moved closer to him. "I'm fine. Do you hear me? I'm fine." She wagged one long finger in his face. "I'm fine."

He did the only thing a red-blooded cowboy could do. He bit her finger.

She jumped back, holding her finger. "You bit me!"

"I'm going to keep biting you until you admit the truth."

"You…you…stay away from my grandmother." She turned and hurried into the living room.

"A thank-you would have been nice!" he shouted to her back.

Miss Bertie walked in and glanced at him, then to the empty doorway. "Is that part of the look?"

Paxton swung toward the door. "No. It's goodbye."

He shoved the shift into gear, backed up and left the crazy ladies behind. He was sticking his nose into something that didn't concern him and he had no desire to get to know Ezra McCray's daughter.

REMI SANK ONTO the sofa, fuming. How dare he stick his nose into her business? She curled her hand into a fist, still feeling the warmth of his lips and his teeth against her skin. That strange gesture had awakened something in her that had been dormant for a long time—the need for male companionship. But not him. He was arrogant and rude and...

Gran sat beside her. "What's the matter, sweetie?"

"Nothing." She tried to hide what she was feeling, but feared she failed.

"What did he mean about a thank-you?"

"Nothing, Gran. He's just an arrogant jerk."

"Oh, I thought he was a very handsome young man. If I were your age, I'd be batting my eyes at him and smiling as sweetly as I could."

"You would not. Things were very proper back then."

Gran let out a big laugh and slapped her leg with her hand. "Oh, sweetie, men and women are men and women at any age. Now your grandpa, he was quiet and shy. I had my work cut out for me because I had him picked out for a long time. We were at a school dance, and when it was time for the girls to choose their partners, I chose him. When they shouted to change partners, I didn't let go and said, 'I'd rather dance with you.' He said, 'I would, too.' And from that day on we were a couple."

"That's so sweet, Gran." How she wished it could be that simple today. But she had too much on her mind to even think about getting involved with someone. Not that he was interested in her. He'd said she was pale and thin. *Pale and thin?* As much as the words made her angry, she knew they were true. Would she ever be strong enough to be able to adopt Annie?

She rested her head on her grandmother's shoulder. "I wish I had lived in your time."

"No, you don't. You're struggling right now, but life will turn around for you. Have you called your parents?"

"Yes. I think they were camped out in my apartment waiting for me to come home."

Gran stroked Remi's hair. "They just worry about you."

"I know, but the accident happened in October and I'm strong enough to live in my apartment again. I wish they would understand that."

"When you're a mother, you'll understand those feelings."

Remi sat up. "I was so devastated when my lawyer called and told me not to go to the hospital anymore to see Annie. The adoption process is in full swing and other couples will be 'visiting' with her, as CPS puts it. When I heard that, I ran like I always do, as if I can outrun my fears. But I have to face that I might not get Annie because of my health. That's so unfair."

"Yes. But you said your interview and the visit to your apartment went well, so don't lose hope."

Remi scooted to face her grandmother. "Dad and Mom moved my bed over and we were able to get Annie's baby bed that Holly and I had bought into the room, and the changing table. A small chest for her clothes fit in there, too. It looks really nice and I was happy the room was big enough. I wish I had had time to get a bigger apartment or maybe a house."

Gran patted Remi's leg. "Love is all that counts."

Remi prayed that was true. "In the fall I go back to teaching and I have to find a really good day care for Annie."

"Now don't go putting the cart before the horse. Let's get over this hurdle first."

"Yes, ma'am." Remi lay back on the couch and raised her left leg. "Time for stretches. Push my leg as far back as you can."

Gran got to her feet. "Oh, Lordy, I hate doing this. I'm afraid I might hurt you and that's…"

Gran's voice faded away as Remi's thoughts turned to Paxton. How odd it was that they'd met on a deserted beach. She'd been running away from her fears. She wondered if he had been, too.

PAXTON DROVE STRAIGHT to the equipment shed to park the trailer. His mother's truck was still at the office so he jumped back into his truck and headed there.

He took one of the leather chairs in front of her desk. She glanced up from the ledger she was writing in. There were several computers in the office, but his mother liked to do things the old way. She wrote things down in the ledger to keep track of cattle and horses and sales and payments.

"How did it go?"

He removed his hat and laid it on the desk. "I didn't know Miss Bertie had a granddaughter—a granddaughter who is Ezra McCray's daughter."

His mother's eyes opened wide. "Remington is here? Bertie must be pleased."

"Remington is her name?" For some reason he found that a little strange. The name didn't fit the feminine woman he'd met.

"Yes, but I think she's called Remi. Ezra named his children Ruger and Remington, after guns. He was one crazy man."

He didn't want to push his privileges as her son, but he had to know. He leaned forward, his hands clasped between his knees. "I don't understand this relationship you have with Miss Bertie. Her daughter was Ezra McCray's wife. And Miss Bertie's much older than you."

She slowly closed the ledger and then glanced at him, her brown eyes dark and serious. "You see, son, Bertie and I have something in common. We both hate the McCrays."

"Yeah. She made that clear."

"To be honest I never thought I'd be friends with Bertie. I met her at one of the Elvis get-togethers some ladies have in town. We found we had a lot to talk about. Bertie and Edgar were devastated when Ava married Ezra. They eloped and they both were of age so there was nothing Bertie or Edgar could do but watch their daughter be brutalized by that horrible man. Time after time Bertie reported Ezra to the sheriff, but Ava would never testify against him."

Paxton listened, and even though it was something he didn't know, what caught his attention were the Elvis get-togethers. "You go to Elvis parties?"

His mother lifted an eyebrow. "Yes, with the sheriff's mother, Mrs. Peabody and several other ladies.

We have a good time. We play poker, listen to music, eat, drink a few beers and talk about the latest gossip in Horseshoe."

"You drink beer?" All his life he'd never seen his mother drink any type of liquor, especially after what had happened to their father. She was against drinking, but she never told any of her sons to stop. They were grown men and she mostly tried to stay out of their lives.

"Is that against the law?"

"No. I'm just surprised."

"You know, son, I'm entitled to get out every once in a while. I enjoy spending time with women with similar interests. We're talking about visiting Graceland in the summer and I'm thinking of going. We need a driver, though. Are you available?" There was a smile in her voice, and he knew she was teasing him.

He shifted uncomfortably, not wanting to say no, but he would rather have his teeth pulled than drive several old ladies to Graceland. Being a dutiful son, he replied, "If you need me to."

His mother laughed, and he realized he hadn't heard her laugh in a long time. She spent all of her time worrying about the ranch and her sons. If she wanted to drink beer and visit Graceland, who was he to judge?

"Don't worry, son. I'm the youngest in the group and I can drive us."

"Are you sure?" He'd try to work it into his schedule if his mother needed him.

"I've hauled cattle all over this country and I think I can get us to Graceland."

"Okay." He stood and pulled five dollars out of his

pocket and laid it on the desk. "From Miss Bertie for gas."

"I forgot to tell you about that. I'm so glad you didn't refuse it."

"Mom, the woman was standing there with a shotgun in her hand. I wasn't going to refuse too much."

"I'm proud of you, son. You're turning into a nice young man. I'm glad you put all that Lisa business behind you."

Lisa? He still hadn't called her, and that was the old Pax, avoiding a confrontation. To be the man he wanted to be, he had to call her and break it off—for good.

He turned to leave the room, but something in him needed to know. "What happened to Miss Bertie's granddaughter? She looks ill."

"I believe she was in a motorcycle accident."

"Motorcycle? I don't see her as a motorcycle chick."

His mother lifted an eyebrow again, which all of her sons knew well. It meant she was either disappointed in what they'd done or what they'd said.

He tried hard not to fidget. "You know what I mean. Piercings, tattoos and leather. This girl is very slight and I can't see her riding a motorcycle."

"It was the boyfriend's, I believe." His mother studied his face and he wanted to squirm again. "Why are you so interested in Remington?"

"I'm not." That was the truth. He was just…curious.

"We just went through this with Phoenix and Rosemary's relationship. Even though I have accepted Rosie, I wouldn't like to see another of my sons getting involved with a McCray."

"Whoa." He held up a hand. "There's nothing like that going on. She's not my type. When she found out I was a Rebel, it was like opening a freezer. Rest assured there's nothing going on. I was just asking."

"Are you sure?"

"Mom."

She got up and walked around her desk to stand in front of him. She lightly touched his face. "I don't think you realize just how handsome you are. This girl is very vulnerable right now and I wouldn't like to see you hurt her in any way. Not that you would intentionally because I know you, and you have a big heart when it counts."

He couldn't believe he was having this conversation with his mother. Avoiding a deep emotional conversation was his top priority when talking to his mother. He didn't know what else to say, except the truth.

"Okay. I promise I won't hurt her. I don't see how that can happen since I've only had one conversation with her. And believe me, I'll never forget that she's Ezra McCray's daughter."

Chapter Three

For the next couple of days Paxton helped on the ranch and worked on his rodeo schedule. He and his friends had ridden in a rodeo in Louisiana and at the Fort Worth Livestock Show and Rodeo. It was now February and he decided not to ride in as many rodeos as he had before. He was getting older and it had taken a toll on his body, so he would ride the big rodeos for the money and for a chance to make it to Las Vegas.

After a hard day of working cattle, he showered and sat on the sofa still going over his schedule. He lived with Jericho in the bunkhouse and they got along well. Jericho never caused trouble and was a good friend to the Rebels.

His brother Egan had met him in prison when Egan had been unjustly accused of a crime. He saved Egan's life and they'd become fast friends. For saving her son's life, their mother had offered him a job on the ranch and he had gladly taken it. He'd grown up on the streets in Houston and had been involved with gangs. But today he was a changed man and the Rebels trusted him completely.

They took turns doing chores around the house. Tonight Rico had kitchen duty. Since they used paper plates for convenience, it was mainly pots, pans and utensils. Pax looked up from his phone and thought he'd talk about something that had been on his mind. He could trust Rico not to say anything.

"I had this strange encounter with a woman."

Rico folded a dishtowel and laid it on the counter. He was well over six feet tall with long hair tied into a ponytail at his neck. A scar was slashed down the side of his face that made him a little off-putting to most. His nationality was a mystery, but Egan had said he was part white, Mexican, black and Indian. He was an intimidating figure.

"You can forget it if you're asking for advice. I don't know a thing about women. I don't think any man does."

"No, I don't want advice. I met this woman while I was in Port Aransas. She was sitting on the beach and couldn't get up so I helped her and that seemed to make her mad. She didn't even say thank you. It was very clear she was ill, but she kept insisting she was fine. Then I went over to haul Miss Bertie's calves and found out she's Miss Bertie's granddaughter. And Ezra McCray's daughter."

"Man, don't you see the sign? Stay Away is blinking in front of you."

"I know. I know. I'm not interested in her or anything. I'm just curious as to why she won't admit she's ill."

"What does it matter?"

Paxton shrugged. "There's just something about her."

"Oh, man, don't you have enough girls chasing you around the rodeo circuit instead of getting involved with someone who's gonna upset your mother?"

"I already told Mom about her."

"What did she say?"

He cleared his throat. "Stay away from her."

"Exactly. Listen to your mother, that's all I'm going to say."

They heard a little voice they knew well—Jake, Phoenix's almost-three-year-old son.

A light tap sounded at the door and reminded Paxton of a rat scratching in a wall. He jumped up and yanked open the door. "Boo," he shouted. Jake stumbled backward, giggling. Then he ran into Paxton's arms, and Paxton swung him up into the air.

"You 'cared me."

He noticed that Jake only had underwear and boots on and it was cold outside. "Where's your clothes, buddy?"

Phoenix and Rosie, who were standing in the doorway, came inside. "Tell him, son."

Jake looked down at his underwear. "I got underwear like Daddy's. I'm a big boy."

"We're potty training," Rosie said. With her red hair and sweet personality, Rosie was a gorgeous woman.

"I wasn't aware Phoenix wore SpongeBob SquarePants underwear."

"Don't start." Over the years, he and Phoenix had teased each other a lot, but of the two of them Phoenix was always the big jokester.

Paxton hugged Jake again. "I'm proud of you, buddy."

Jake hugged him back. "Me big boy now." Jake noticed Rico and held out his arms. Rico took him. "Lookie, Rico." Jake pointed to his underwear.

"I see, big boy."

Jake smiled. "Gotta go show Grandma." He wiggled down and ran to Phoenix.

"We have to put on your coat," Phoenix said.

"He wouldn't wear his clothes." Rosie helped Jake with his coat. "He wants everybody to see his underwear."

Jake waved goodbye and Phoenix closed the door.

"Do you ever think of having kids, Rico?"

"Nah. I'm content the way I am."

"I always thought I wouldn't want kids. They're a lot of work, but every time I hold Jake I get this feeling that it would be great to have a kid."

Rico sank into his recliner. "That shouldn't be much of a problem for you."

"I want to fall in love first."

Rico clicked on the TV. "Now that could be a problem."

"You don't think I can fall in love?"

"I think this discussion has gone on long enough." He turned up the TV, and Paxton walked into his room. His cell buzzed with a message. He looked at the name. *Lisa.*

It was time to cowboy-up and do the right thing—the mature thing. He touched her name and her cell rang. She answered right away.

"Oh, teddy bear, I knew you'd call. I knew you'd realize we belong together."

"No, that's not why I'm calling." He took a deep breath. "I thought you would get the message if I didn't answer your calls, but evidently the message has eluded you. When we broke up two years ago, it was final. It's still final for me."

"I know I was a bitch back then, but I've changed and I know what I want. I want you in my life."

"I'm sorry, Lisa. That's not going to happen."

"Have you found someone else?"

He started to lie and put an end to this. But again, that would be the old Paxton and he was working very hard to change his bad habits. "No. It's just the way I feel. Please don't call me again."

"Paxton, baby. You don't mean that."

"Goodbye, Lisa. I wish you the best." He clicked off and blocked her number from his phone. It was over and it wasn't as bad as he'd thought it would be. Maybe he should buy some SpongeBob SquarePants underwear, too.

THE NEXT MORNING in the office, Falcon was doling out orders.

"Mr. Busby wants ten heifers. He picked them out two days ago. Elias was with me so he'll remember which heifers to load."

"What?" Elias sat up straight in his chair.

"Those heifers we looked at the other day with Mr. Busby. Did you lose your memory?"

"Oh, yeah. Got it." Paxton knew Elias and he knew every cow and calf on the ranch. He was just jacking with Falcon. Elias leaned over and whispered loudly to Paxton, "All heifers look alike, right?"

"You're an idiot."

Their mother's cell rang before Falcon could figure out what Elias was saying. She clicked off and looked at Quincy. "That was Miss Bertie. She wants to know if you can help her with a cow whose udder is too big for the calf to suck. It was born last night and she's wants to get it to the pen, but the cow keeps charging her."

"I don't mind helping Miss Bertie, Mom," Quincy said. "But I don't want to get too far away from Jenny. Her dad and sister are over there now and she made me leave the house for a while. I want to be nearby in case she goes into premature labor."

Paxton stood. "I'll go."

Everyone, including Elias, who had his hat pulled over his face and was teetering on the two back legs of his chair, looked at him. Grandpa's mouth fell open and everyone seemed to be speechless.

"What? I can't be neighborly and helpful?"

"It's just something we've never seen before," Egan said.

"Kind of like Phoenix doing a full day's work. It's just something you don't see too often." Elias was always cruising for a fight, but today he wasn't going to get one.

Phoenix threw his arm around Elias's shoulders. "And like Elias being stone-cold sober all day."

"Enough with the joking around." Falcon frowned. "We have work to do. Paxton will help Miss Bertie and the rest of you will saddle up and bring those heifers to the corral to load. Elias and Jude will deliver them. After that, there's feeding to do."

His brothers filed out of the office. Falcon followed, still dishing out orders. As Rico passed Paxton, he slapped him on the back. "Didn't see the sign, did you?"

No one heard Rico but Paxton. He knew he was acting out of character, but he was going to get her sea-green eyes out of his head. One more encounter should do it.

"Want me to go with you?" Grandpa asked. "I've known Bertie all my life and she's a handful. Always was. In school she was tough as leather and still is. But boy, she could dance the soles right off her shoes."

"I got it, Grandpa, but thanks."

Grandpa slowly pushed to his feet, and Paxton noticed, maybe for the first time, that Grandpa was slowing down. It was hard to see someone you love getting older, but Grandpa had so much vinegar in him he was going to last a long time.

"Good. I'm going over to see Jenny."

"Abe, don't you think you bother them enough? Let Jenny rest." It was well-known that their mother and grandfather didn't get along and it was a strain on all of them, but somehow they managed to live on the same property and keep the anger from boiling over. It had to do with their father's death. They blamed each other when the only person to blame was John Rebel himself. Paxton didn't want to think about his father and quickly switched his thoughts to the conversation at hand.

"I can visit Jenny anytime I want."

"Suit yourself."

Grandpa stomped out.

His mother glanced at him. "Thank you, son, for helping. I appreciate it. You might take a horse. Bertie doesn't have one anymore."

"I will."

"Son?"

He turned back.

"This isn't about the granddaughter, is it?"

He looked into his mom's worried eyes and something like fear uncurled in his stomach. "Why are you so worried about me and Remi?"

She shrugged. "I don't know. You're just so charming and girls fall for you."

He didn't know what to say to that, but he was old enough to make his own decisions, even though it might disappoint his mother.

Chapter Four

When Paxton crossed the cattle guard with the trailer clanging behind him, first thing he noticed was Remi standing at the edge of the corral. She seemed to be holding on to it, huddled in a blue coat with the hood over her head. Much as the first time he'd seen her. Her dog was at her feet.

In the distance near a pond he could see Miss Bertie with a stick in her hand trying to shoo a red-and-white-faced cow with a baby calf toward the pen, but she wasn't having any luck.

He parked the truck and got out. Remi came toward him, holding on to the dog's collar. It hit him for the first time that she used the dog for balance.

"Could you please help my grandmother? The cow is going to hurt her and she won't listen to me. She's so stubborn."

He tipped his hat. "It must be genetic."

"What do you mean by that?" Her eyes narrowed.

He unlatched the trailer gate with more force than necessary and then pulled the ramp down so he could unload Romeo. A few years ago Falcon had bought several young geldings and Egan and Jude had broken them. They both had a soft voice that animals reacted to. Paxton liked the chestnut-colored horse with a white blaze on his face and had asked to keep it. Phoenix had named it Romeo and it had stuck. He had turned out to be a great quarter horse.

Paxton placed his boot in the stirrup and swung into the saddle. Mostly, he was avoiding answering her question. "Whatever you want it to mean," he replied, and rode toward Miss Bertie.

"How rude." Remi watched him ride away and had the urge to throw something at his straight back. But her temper soon cooled as she continued to watch him. He had to be the most handsome cowboy she'd ever seen. The most handsome man, too. He was rugged, strong and charismatic in a way she couldn't explain because most of the time she just wanted to smack him. Maybe because he reminded her of things she'd forgotten—the touch of a man, the feel of a man's hands on her body and a masculine scent that took her away to a beautiful place. It had all been snatched from her and she would never...

She shook her head. What was she doing? She couldn't go back so she had to go forward. But just looking at Mr. Paxton Rebel made her aware that she was still very much alive.

He rode up to her grandmother and they were talking, but it seemed more like they were arguing. Her grandmother waved the stick at him and then stomped to the corral with Memphis on her heels. Remi's eyes were glued to the cowboy and she wondered what he'd do to get the cow in the pen.

He removed a rope from the saddle horn and made a

large loop. Swinging it above his head, he rode toward the cow, yelling, "Hi ya! Hi ya!"

The cow threw up her head, refusing to budge. He popped her with the rope and she spun in a circle and tried to charge him, but once again he stung her with the rope. The cow licked the calf and slowly started walking toward the corral. Halfway there she turned and tried to charge the horse, but the cowboy used the rope to guide the cow toward the open gate that Gran was holding.

Once the cow and calf were inside, Gran closed the gate, and the cowboy dismounted and jumped across the fence as if it was no more than a twig.

Gran shook the stick at him. "Let me tell you something, sonny boy, no man tells me what to do."

"Yes, ma'am." His voice was laced with sarcasm, but Gran didn't seem to notice. She was intent on doing things her way.

"Good. Now let's take care of this cow. Remi, open the chute."

What! To do that she would have to climb over the fence and she knew she couldn't. What did she do?

She looked up and stared into the cowboy's dark caramel eyes and saw his concern for her.

"I got it. I'm closer." He marched over and opened the chute, inches away from her.

"Thank you," she breathed hoarsely.

"Aw. The lady knows the words." The corners of his mouth turned into a smile and it was lethal to her emotional state. Her heart raced and her hands were clammy. Suddenly, she was hot. She pushed the hood from her head and unbuttoned her coat. She'd never had this experience before and she rather liked it. Only for a moment. She couldn't be attracted to Paxton Rebel.

"Are you gonna help me or what?" Gran shouted.

In minutes they had the cow in the chute, and Paxton shoved the little calf in butt-first so he was facing the udder. It was swollen and the teats stuck out filled with milk.

Gran had a stool and a bucket and began to milk the cow. It sounded like rain on a tin roof. Paxton slid into the chute with the calf. Once the teats were smaller Paxton pushed the calf's face toward the udder. The little thing searched for food, but still wasn't latching on.

Paxton looked at her. "Reach in and pull a teat toward his mouth."

"Huh. Okay." She reached into the space between the boards and found a teat. It felt like a tight rubber glove filled with water.

"Squeeze it into his mouth," Paxton said.

"I don't know how to milk."

"Just squeeze it."

She did and milk squirted onto the calf's face and he stuck his tongue out. She squeezed it again, and he caught the teat and began to suck.

"He's sucking!" she shouted, excited. The calf was in full control so she let go and stroked his head and back. "He's so cute. His red hair even has a curl to it. I think I'll call him Curly."

"We're not naming this calf," Gran snapped. "You don't name animals you plan to sell, and this one will be sold in the fall to help pay taxes."

"Oh, Gran."

Gran stood, shaking her head. "City girls. You just can't change 'em. Now I'm going to the house to fix lunch. We'll have hot biscuits and gravy and fried chicken. Remi, help Handsome finish up. There's square bales in the barn. Give her enough to keep her happy."

Paxton opened the chute and the cow backed out, the little calf following her, eager to suck.

"It's barely nine o'clock. Why is she fixing lunch so early?" He leaped over the fence and stood next to her, within touching distance. The cold air was suddenly warm. Too warm.

Her throat went dry. "She, uh, has to kill a chicken first and take the feathers off and whatever."

"You're kidding. Nobody does that anymore. I remember my grandma doing that when I was kid, but I thought these days everyone got their chicken at the grocery store or already fried at the chicken place."

"Gran does everything from scratch, the old way."

"Well, I don't have time to stay for lunch. I have work to do at the ranch." He started toward the barn and then stopped. "I thought you were supposed to help."

"Oh, oh." She walked toward him, holding on to Sadie, not knowing what she could do to help him.

Paxton nodded toward the dog. "You use her for balance, don't you?"

She refused to answer as she followed him into the barn. A pungent hay scent filled the air. He cut the strings on a bale and gathered a block in his hands.

"I'd ask you to carry this, but I know you can't."

"You don't have to be mean about it."

He sighed. "I'm not. I'm just curious as to why you don't want your grandmother to know you're not as strong as you should be." He walked out of the barn with the hay and she followed more slowly. Leaning on the fence, she watched as he laid the hay on the ground. The cow immediately began to eat.

She loved watching him. His actions were effortless and she knew the muscles beneath his winter coat had to be custom-made from hard work. Gran had said that he was a bull rider. To do that he had to stay in shape and just looking at him she knew that he did.

A honking sound echoed through the landscape and Remi looked up to see Canada geese landing on the pond. "Look, geese." She slowly headed toward the pond and Paxton caught up with her.

"What's so special about the geese?"

She sat on the small weather-worn bench Gran had put there to sit and feed the geese and ducks. Paxton sat beside her. Maybe just a little too close. Hay, milk and the musky scent of male surrounded her. She didn't know why she was so aware of him and she had to stop torturing herself.

"It's nice out here by the pond," he said.

Large live oak trees shaded the pond on the right, their heavy branches just inches from the water. The air was fresh and invigorating. A peacefulness came over Remi.

"Yes, it's nice." Her eyes met the caramel sweetness of his and she knew she was fighting a losing battle.

Finally, he asked again, "What's so special about the geese?"

She pointed to two geese on the other side of the pond. "That's Henry and Henrietta, otherwise known as Henny."

"It looks like one of them has a broken wing. It's almost dragging the ground."

"That's Henny. Gran said a bobcat attacked her, but she managed to get away. She can't fly anymore so this is home now. Gran was worried Henry would fly away and leave Henny here by herself, but Henry has never left her side. Canada geese mate for life. Isn't that wonderful?"

"Unbelievable."

She scooted a little farther away from him. He was so close she was feeling breathless. "Yeah. It would be nice if humans could get it right, but there's more divorce now than ever."

"Mmm." He leaned forward, his hands clasped between his knees. "I don't want to be nosy, but what happened to you?"

"It's a long story." She ran her hand down the thigh of her jogging pants and wondered if he was someone she could confide in.

"I got time."

"You said earlier you had to work," she reminded him.

"Aw, that's just to get away from Miss Bertie. She's a character."

"Yes, but she can be lovable, too."

"I'll take your word for that."

The geese squawked on the pond, flapping their wings and ducking their heads into the water. It was peaceful and comforting and she felt as if they were the only two people in the world.

"So what happened?" He was prodding her, but in a nice way.

"My parents are very protective of me. It's smothering sometimes. I wasn't even two years old when my mom left Horseshoe and she didn't come back for a whole year. Gran came to see us in Houston and she complained all the time that it was ridiculous Mom couldn't bring me to visit her. Eventually we started visiting, but we never left the ranch. I guess my mom was afraid of running into Uncle Ira. They had a big fight over Ruger. It even went to court, and since Ruger was eleven, the judge let him decide where he wanted to live and he chose my uncle. My mom was devastated. I've called Ruger many times and he's always tells me to stay away. He's my brother and I'd like to have some sort of connection with him, but Uncle Ira controls him."

She took a deep breath and realized she was rambling on like a girl on a first date.

"So your relationship with your brother and the rest of the family is strained."

"Yes, you could say that." She watched the geese play on the water. "My mom remarried two years later, and Nathan Roberts adopted me. He's the only dad I've ever known. My mom refuses to talk about Ezra McCray. Everything I know I've learned from Gran and she tends to exaggerate. I do know he wasn't a very nice person, though, because he beat my mother."

"Everything I've heard is bad, too, so maybe you were better off not knowing him."

She turned to look at him. "Does it feel strange for you and me to be talking?"

"No. Why?"

"Your father killed my biological father."

"That could be a stumbling block, but it was a tragedy and it's in the past. That's the way I look at it. I mean, I didn't kill your father and you didn't kill my father. I think it's time for everyone to move on."

"Yeah." She kicked at the grass with her sneaker. "It's hard sometimes and I know my mother thinks about it constantly. She hates visiting Horseshoe, but I'm happy she allowed me to come and stay with Gran during the summers. I'm glad I know my grandmother, even if she's a little eccentric."

"Is that what she is?" His lips twitched into a smile and she found herself smiling back.

"Yes, she is, and she likes you, so count that as a blessing."

"It's hard to believe Miss Bertie and my mom are friends. I didn't even know about the Elvis club."

"I think it's nice to stay young in your heart."

"Mmm. I think the feud is fading in some ways."

"Why do you say that?" she asked.

"My brother Phoenix married Rosemary McCray in December."

"Gran told me and I thought it was awesome. She also said that Uncle Ira had disowned Rosemary."

"Yes. He married her off to a man twice her age and he abused her. Finally she had the courage to get out and make a life for herself, and still Ira wouldn't accept her back into the family."

"She's my first cousin and I'd love to meet her. Gran said I have lots of cousins and I haven't met any of them."

"I can tell you for certain that Rosie—that's what everyone calls her—would love to meet you. She's that kind of person, sweet, loving and giving. And beautiful."

"Do you have a crush on her?"

He laughed out loud and the sound echoed through the trees. The geese squawked and flapped around in the water at the interruption. It was in the forties, but his laugh warmed her through and through.

"The Rebel boys made a pact a long time ago to stay away from each other's girlfriends. Actually, it was something our father told us to do—to never go against our brothers."

He scooted on the bench to face her. "I think you're avoiding telling me what happened to you. You've talked around it, but you haven't actually said why you're so weak."

She clasped her hands in her lap. "Maybe because it makes me sound impulsive and immature."

He poked a finger into his chest. "You're looking at Mr. Immature."

"I can't believe that. You always seem so confident and in control."

"Oh, man, I used to think that way, too. There's nothing like being knocked off my pedestal. I've led a pretty selfish life riding the rodeo circuit, drinking and partying. And then there were the girls."

"I can imagine."

"Okay, don't get snotty. What I'm going to tell you is going to change the way you think of me."

"How do you know I think about you?" She blinked. "Oh, you think I might have a crush on you because every girl you meet does."

He frowned. "No, it's not that. It's about immaturity. My immaturity."

She settled back and listened.

"I had this high school girlfriend and we dated for years and then I started riding the circuit and we didn't see each other that often. And then there were a lot of girls all chasing after me. I cheated on Jenny and slept with other girls. I felt bad about it and told her and you know what she did?"

"I don't have a clue."

"She forgave me."

"She must really love you to be that forgiving."

"I lost my father about the same time Jenny lost her mother and we had a connection because of that. We consoled each other and cried together, but it wasn't love. Jenny and I were just best friends. I met this actress in Los Angeles and I asked her to marry me. And I didn't tell Jenny. She was devastated with the news. I was a jackass because I couldn't tell her the truth."

"You're a jerk."

His eyes crinkled mischievously. "Oh, but this has a happy ending."

Was he married? She hadn't even thought of that. She'd swallowed hard. "She forgave you again."

"No. There's just so much a woman will take and Jenny had reached her limit. My brother Quincy was there to console her."

"I thought you said the Rebel boys didn't—"

"Yeah, but in this instance it was right. They fell in love, and when I found out, I acted like a fool and hit Quincy. Now, if you knew Quincy you'd know he has a soft heart, but he wasn't going to walk away and let me have Jenny. The truth is Jenny didn't want me anymore and I realized I didn't want her, either. We just kept holding on to that relationship for some reason and it wasn't working. We both knew that and we finally said goodbye. Quincy and Jenny got married and they're expecting their first child in March."

The relief she felt at his words was insane. Why would she care that he wasn't married? She couldn't imagine any woman giving up Paxton, though. He was just too charming and handsome. But what woman enjoyed being cheated on? Remi certainly didn't. Her dream man was a cad. And a Rebel.

He leaned closer. "So, you see, I win on the immaturity thing, but I've turned over a new leaf and I'm trying to make better decisions for the future. Do you think a bad boy can change?"

She met the gleam in his eyes with a strength she didn't know she possessed. There was something about the mischief deep in his eyes that changed her whole way of thinking. But she had enough sense not to let it show.

"No."

Chapter Five

The word slid across Paxton's cheek like a chunk of ice. Cold. Cold. Cold. The woman didn't have a sense of humor.

"Hey, I was just kidding."

"I wasn't." The temperature of her voice dropped another degree.

He studied her face, the tight lips and the frosty eyes. "You really believe the guy who helped you to your feet in Port Aransas is a bad guy?"

"I think you're a charmer and a ladies' man."

"Listen, I know I've lived a rough life, but I'm trying to change. I would think you'd at least give me the benefit of the doubt."

"What does it matter what I think? We'll never see each other again."

She was right. What did it matter?

"You're right. We're two strangers talking, but I've been doing most of the talking. You've talked about everything except what happened to you. What happened?"

She wrapped her arms around her waist as if to ward off the memories.

"I know it was a motorcycle accident." He didn't

know why he was pushing it, but he wanted her to talk and share something about her life.

Her eyes were enormous in her pale face. "How do you know that?"

He saw no reason not to be honest. "My mother told me."

"You asked or was it a topic of conversation?"

He rubbed his hands together. "I asked because I was curious as to why a girl stubbornly refuses to admit she's not completely well."

She pulled her coat tighter around her. "You know, you're very pushy."

"And charming." He smiled his best smile and her lips twitched. Maybe she did have a sense of humor.

"Mmm. It's a long story and you said you have to get back to work."

He stretched out his legs and crossed his boots at the ankles. "I've decided to take some time."

"You're not going to stop, are you?"

"Probably not."

"Since you were so nice opening the chute and helping me in Port Aransas, I'll tell you. But I want you to know I'm not completely stupid. I had my phone and was going to call the hotel to ask for help."

"That's good to know." But his guess was she would have struggled for hours before doing that.

"I told you my parents are very protective. They don't seem to think I can live my life on my own and I've tried hard to be independent. I have my own apartment, a good job, and I don't take any money from them. But they still can't help trying to take care of me."

She shoved her hands into her pockets as if the next part was difficult. "I was dating this guy, Chuck, and my parents didn't like him. We were arguing about it one day at my apartment when I was getting ready to go out with him. Finally, I ran out the door and jumped on the back of his motorcycle and we sped off—to hell."

She drew a deep breath. "Riding away I felt selfish and immature like a fifteen-year-old. Instead of talking to my parents like an adult, I was running away. I wanted to go back and apologize. That's when I smelled the pot. I asked Chuck to stop so I could get off. He just laughed."

She took another quick breath. "It started to rain and the motorcycle hit a patch of oil and hydroplaned. All I remember was the screaming and the pain. I woke up in a hospital a week later with my Mom, Dad and Gran around my bed. They looked so worried and I didn't understand what was going on for a second and then it all came rushing back."

He waited for her to continue, but she didn't. She seemed locked in that moment as if she was reliving all the pain and he hated now that he had pushed her.

"You don't have to tell me anymore," he said quietly.

She shook her head. "No, it's okay. I just have these waves of thinking maybe I do need my parents to watch over me. And then I remember I'm a grown woman and I can't stay their little girl forever. I have to live my own life even if I make big mistakes. And I'm paying for that mistake."

She took a moment. "When I learned about my injuries, I couldn't believe it. I had a broken collarbone, a fractured arm, my ribs were fractured. There were internal injuries, too. But the worst injury was to my left leg. The motorcycle landed on my leg, burned and crushed my knee. The surgeon wanted to amputate above the knee and my father, who's a hospital administrator, called in a more qualified orthopedic surgeon. He did a total knee replacement and ran a rod up my thighbone and into my shinbone to hold the knee in place. It worked and I'd never been so happy in my whole life."

She paused again. "A lot of the muscle above my knee was gone and we waited to see if more tissue would grow back. Some did. They did skin grafts to help close the wound. Then I had to wait for the wound to heal. After many weeks, they finally stood me up. It was painful, but I made myself do it. Every day I got a little better and I kept hoping I would one day be back to normal. I'd gotten a miracle and I was grateful for that. I knew my leg would never be the way it was, but at least I had my leg. I will never be able to wear a bathing suit or high heels or shorts again, though."

"Does that matter?"

She lifted an eyebrow. "To an almost-twenty-eight-year-old woman it does. But I can't go back and change things so I have to accept the way things are."

He reached out to touch her cheek. She didn't pull away or seem infuriated that he dared to touch her. It was just an impulse and in her eyes he saw she understood. "I think you're awesome with or without high heels or skimpy shorts."

"You're flirting." Her lips turned into a refreshing smile.

"Yeah." He sat up straight. "I'm a master at that."

"Mmm." A flurry of honking made her look toward the pond, where the geese were beginning to fight. "Henry's letting them know he's boss." The geese flapped their wings, batting at each other like boxers, stirring up the water.

Paxton watched them for a minute, until Henry swam to shore to sit near Henny. "I'm sorry for everything you've had to go through."

"Thank you," she murmured, not looking at him.

"I'm still curious about a couple of things. Why are your parents so protective of you?"

"When my mom left Horseshoe with me, she was so afraid Uncle Ira would try to kidnap me because he refused to let Ruger go with us. I think she still fears one day he'll take me away from her like he did my brother."

"After all these years, I doubt it."

"My mom and I don't talk about it anymore. She gets so upset as I don't agree with her point of view. I didn't live through all the pain and I tell her all the time that I'm an adult now and I can stay or go anywhere I want."

"Good for you."

The wind had picked up and again she gathered her coat closer around her. "Did I answer all your questions?" she asked mischievously.

It was good to see her in a better mood and her smile was infectious, making him forget what he wanted to ask her. Almost. "No. I still don't understand why it's hard for you to admit you're not completely well."

She shifted nervously on the bench. "I told you it was a long story."

"I'm listening."

"My best friend was Holly. We went to grade school and high school together, but we went to different colleges and lost touch for a while. She got married and I was dating. After college I started applying for jobs, and I got one at a small private school as a pre-K teacher. It was ironic that Holly was also a pre-K teacher in that same school. We were so excited to see each other again and became inseparable. Her husband was in the marines and was gone all the time. We spent most evenings together going over our classroom plans or going out to eat or walking for exercise. I helped her decorate a nursery and she was ecstatic that Derek was going to come home for the birth."

Remi took a long breath. "When I was in the hospital, she came every day to see me. I went home the day before Thanksgiving and she still came all the way out to my parents' house to visit. Then one day she didn't come. I thought she had to run errands or something. The next day she didn't come, either, and I asked my mom to check on her. My mom and dad walked into my room and I knew something was wrong by the expressions on their faces. My mom said Holly had died."

She bit her lip and then continued. "Derek had been killed on his last mission in Afghanistan. When Holly got the news, she collapsed and went into labor. There were complications after delivering the baby, and she died. But then there was the baby. She was going to name her Anne, and call her Annie, after her mother, who had passed away when Holly was ten. The baby—" she took a gulp of air "—had a congenital heart defect that required surgery. I was there every day for Annie because I knew Holly would want me to be. I sat in a chair by her incubator and talked to her and told her about her parents and how much they loved and wanted her."

She gulped another breath. "Then one day a lady from Child Protective Services came to speak to me. She said since they couldn't find a relative to take Annie, she'd become a ward of the state and they were putting her up for adoption. At that moment I knew I wanted to be Annie's mother. Holly would have wanted that and I told the lady so. I contacted an attorney and filled out the appropriate forms, but my attorney told me not to get my hopes up because CPS was going to look at everything, especially my health. I would have to be completely well and able to care for Annie. The only problem was Annie got well before I did. I'm still in therapy and I didn't want anyone at the hospital to know that. So I say I'm fine. I have to be. I can't lose Annie."

Paxton now understood and wanted to take her in his arms and hold her. He'd never seen such a fighting spirit in one person. Not only was she fighting for herself, but for a little girl who needed a home.

Before he could say anything, she started speaking again. "They've started the adoption process and my lawyer got a call from CPS. They asked for me to stay away from the hospital for a few days because couples were going to be visiting with Annie. You see, Annie already knows me and she gets excited when she sees me."

"Can't they see that?" he asked.

"It doesn't matter. I have to be healthy to be a mother, as I'm told. I'm doing everything I can to make that happen, but I'm so afraid they'll give Annie to someone else."

He leaned forward, his eyes on her. "Are you prepared for that?"

She shook her head. "No, I'm not. I know in my heart that Annie belongs with me."

"I don't know much about Child Protective Services or adoption. But I do know they always try to place kids into a happy home and that usually includes a couple. Sometimes that's not completely true, but—"

"I have to get Annie," she said in a plaintive voice that gnawed at his insides. "She's the child of my heart and the only child I'll ever have."

That threw him. "What are you talking about?"

She raised her head, her eyes sad, but there was strength behind all the sadness. "The accident took that from me, too. I'll never be able to have a child of my own."

Oh, man. This was out of his realm of expertise. He didn't know how to help her and it surprised him that he wanted to. But the magic words eluded him.

She brushed back her short hair. "So you don't have to worry about me falling for you. That won't happen with you or any other man."

She had stunned him with her openness and he had no idea what to say. He had never talked to someone with this kind of problem before and a rawness ached in his gut at his ineptness. To break the awkward moment he said the only thing that came into his mind. "Why are you here at your gran's instead of in therapy?"

She huddled deeper in her coat as the wind grew chilly. "Well, I can't be at the hospital, and I wanted to get my thoughts straight. Gran's is my happy place. I brought my stationary bike and I still do all my exercises and stretches to continue my therapy. I will never stop that."

It occurred to him that if other couples were seeing the child, there was a good chance Remi wasn't going to get custody. She needed to be prepared. That was what the fear he saw in her eyes in Port Aransas was about—the fear of losing Annie.

She'd been through so much and still had hurdles

to get over, but at the end she was hoping a little girl would be waiting for her. But…

"I may be out of line, but are you prepared to be a single mom?"

She stood up and glared at him. "You don't think I would make a good mother?"

"I'm not saying that."

"It is. You're saying they're not going to choose me as the mother because of my health?"

He didn't know how to tell her other than to be truthful. "I'm saying you need to think about it."

"I have, Paxton, and I'll never believe Annie won't be my daughter one day." She got up and walked as quickly as she was able toward the house. She was running away from him. Sadie trotted beside her and he followed more slowly.

Halfway to the house she fell. He ran to help her, but stopped. Remi needed help but she was so proud. He stood there wondering what to do and wondering how he got mixed up in all this. In her life. In her problems. In her pain. He took a deep breath and glanced to the left and saw a tree branch had fallen from an oak tree. He remembered when he was a kid and his grandmother had broken her ankle. She'd walked with a boot and a cane until it had healed.

He broke off a limb and fished his pocket knife out of his jeans. Grandpa had taught all of his grandsons how to use one. "You can't whittle unless your knife is sharp," Grandpa had said. Paxton's knife was always razor sharp.

Carving off an end to make it smooth, he watched Remi. She wiped away tears and every time she did his gut tightened into a knot and he had trouble breathing.

He hated to see her in so much pain. Especially because he had caused some of it.

Scraping off the bark, he gave her time to cool down. He kept whittling until he had both ends smooth and the center trimmed and as clean as he could get it. He walked over to her.

She stuck out her arms. "Go away, Paxton, and leave me alone."

He knelt in front of her. "I'm not going anywhere. I want you to understand that I think you would make the perfect mother for Annie, but I want you to be prepared to face whatever happens. That's all I was saying."

"I'm sorry. I just get emotional about Annie." She wiped her cheeks with the backs of her hands. "What's that?" She pointed to the stick in his hand.

"It's a stick I cut from the oak tree."

"I can see that. What's it for?"

"I want you to try something for me."

"What?"

"Just don't say no."

She took a moment to think about it. "Okay."

He scooted a little closer. "I want you to get your right leg under you and your left leg as close as you can and then I want you to put both hands on the stick and push down and lift yourself up from the ground."

The wind ruffled her hair and her eyes grew enormous. "You think I can do that?"

"Without a doubt." He smiled and, as in times past, he hoped it would work.

The winter leaves swirled around them as she took her time to think. "Okay." She slipped out of her jacket, leaned forward and put both hands on the cold ground and got her right leg beneath her. Her left leg stuck out to the side at a ninety-degree angle.

"Lean in and put both of your hands on the stick." He placed it in front of her. "One above the other and grip tightly and then push down with all of your strength."

She did as he'd said.

"On the count of three I want you to push. One. Two. Three."

Her face scrunched into a frown and her arms tightened with all her strength and she pushed down. Paxton held his breath. But like magic she stood up. "I did it! I did it, Paxton!" She dropped the stick and threw her arms around his waist and rested her head on his chest, trembling from head to toe.

His left arm went around her waist to hold her steady and his right hand cradled her head. The moment she rested her head on his chest something happened inside him. He was trying to understand it. Somehow his heart had opened up and he'd let Remi inside. He'd never let anyone get that close, not even Lisa, and he had been prepared to marry her.

When his dad had died he'd closed his heart with a steel door that no one could ever open. He never wanted to live through that kind of pain again. It was probably the main reason for his drinking, the girls and the parties. It was easy that way. His emotions weren't involved.

But standing in the cold wind holding Remi, he wanted to protect her, to take care of her and to be there for her always. It was a strange feeling for a man who'd always lived for himself and a good time. And Remi wasn't his type. He liked blondes—voluptuous blondes. But the small fragile woman leaning against him seemed to have some kind of hold over him.

She wasn't fragile, though. She had more strength than anyone he'd ever met. She was a bundle of fire, energy and femininity that echoed through his male body.

The power of his feelings scared him. He never felt this way about a woman before. His instincts told him to run. But he didn't want to hurt Remi…and he'd promised his mother.

His conflicting thoughts went around and around in his head. Remi had problems and he wasn't the type of man to handle life's difficulties well. But then again, what did it matter when the heart was involved? He'd wanted to change, but he wasn't sure he could change that much and be the man Remi needed. Not that she wanted him, but with a little effort on his part he knew their relationship could get serious. Did he run? Or did he stay?

The trembling in Remi subsided and she leaned back, her eyes sparkling as bright as any stars he'd ever seen. "I did it. Do you know what that means?"

That you're burrowing so deep into my heart that I may never get you out.

"I'm guessing it has something to do with Annie."

"Yes." She caught the lapel of his jacket and pulled his head down to hers. Her lips touched his with a fire that blazed through his body. "Thank you for giving me the courage to get up off the ground and get on with my life. If I did it once, I can do it again. And again. That means I'm improving and my chances of getting Annie are better." She smiled at him so sweetly that he was completely lost in feelings he wanted to deny, but he kept staring into her shining eyes. Running didn't seem an option anymore.

She reached down and picked up the stick. "I'm going to keep this forever."

"Have you ever thought of using a cane?"

"Yes," she answered with a bashful grin. "But the vanity thing got in the way. I didn't want to look like an old woman. I mean, what guy would look at a woman with a cane?"

"Do you want guys to look at you?" he asked with a touch of jealousy, which shocked him.

"Well, no. Even though I'm not ready to get involved with anyone, I'm still a young woman. But my whole life is centered around Annie and her future."

"What about your future?" He was pushing her again, but he had this need for her to look at him and see him as a man, and not just a ladies' man.

She placed her hand on his chest, and he felt the warmth through his shirt. "You just made my life so much better. Thank you. Now I have to get back to Houston and Annie."

That took him by surprise. "You're leaving?"

"It's been days since I've seen Annie and I have to get back to her."

"Didn't they ask you to stay away?"

A tinge of pink colored her cheeks as she slipped on her jacket. "I'll get around that." She started walking toward the house, saying over her shoulder, "We better go. I bet Gran's waiting on us."

He stared at her back. Sadie was on one side and Remi used the stick on the other as she walked. She was leaving without a backward glance. So much for his ladies' man status. She'd opened his heart and slammed it shut faster than he could blink. He took a deep breath of cold air and let it circulate through his system. It was just as well things ended now. What he was feeling for Remi was just a result of his conflicting thoughts about his future. It had been on his mind so much and he'd reached out to her for a reason he didn't understand just yet. But for now the "The Heartthrob" was headed back to the rodeo circuit. His heart intact.

Chapter Six

When Paxton reached the back gate, he'd come to terms with whatever he was feeling for Remi. He'd forgotten for a brief moment she was Ezra McCray's daughter and that was a big stumbling block for him and the whole family. He had plans to meet friends in Houston on Saturday and it was time for him to move on and forget this little interlude.

Remi held the gate open, holding Memphis by the collar. "If I let her out, she'll just chase the chickens and geese and then Gran will get mad."

After closing the gate, he followed her inside. She was so happy she seemed to be bouncing on the balls of her feet.

"Gran, the most amazing thing happened," Remi said even before they could get inside the back door.

Miss Bertie turned from the sink. "Where have you two been? I've been calling and calling."

"We were talking."

"You were talking and couldn't hear me hollering?"

"We were down by the pond watching the geese." Remi waved a hand. "Listen, Gran, I have something to tell you."

Miss Bertie placed her hands on her hips. "Something amazing, you said."

"I fell…"

"Oh, my goodness." Miss Bertie ran to Remi and patted her shoulders and arms. "Did you hurt yourself?"

"No." She held up the stick. "Paxton made me this and I pushed up from the ground all by myself. Paxton didn't help me at all, did you?" She looked at Pax.

"No. She did it all by herself." He removed his hat and coat.

"I thought you could get up off the floor and were just doing strengthening and stretches." Miss Bertie stared at Remi.

Remi looked down at the cane in her hand. "No, Gran. I'm not quite there yet."

Miss Bertie hugged Remi. "Don't you think I know that? I was just waiting for you to tell me something."

"I'm sorry. I just want everyone to think I'm well so it won't affect the adoption."

"I'm your grandma. You can tell me anything."

"Thanks, Gran. But I think it's time to go. I have to get back to Annie."

Miss Bertie stepped back with a frown. "You're not going anywhere. Those people asked you to stay away so potential adoptive parents could visit with Annie and that's what you're going to do. You're going to follow the rules. What do you think those nurses are going to tell CPS about you coming in when you're not supposed to? It won't be good and it will go against you."

Sighing deeply, Remi complained, "Oh, Gran. Why do you have to be so sensible?"

Miss Bertie glanced to the table. "Sit down and let's

have lunch." She pointed to a chair at the end of the table. "You sit there, Handsome."

Paxton took a seat and Remi removed her coat and sat down, some of the happiness leaving her face. It was clear how much she loved that little girl.

On the table sat Elvis salt and pepper shakers and a napkin holder. Elvis was everywhere in this kitchen. He hadn't noticed before. He stared at all the food—fried chicken, gravy, mashed potatoes, biscuits and green beans. A pie was cooling on the counter. He'd need a nap after eating a meal like this.

As he buttered a biscuit, Miss Bertie eyed him. "You know, Handsome, you remind me a lot of Abe."

"My grandfather?"

"Yes, sir. Old Abe was a handsome devil back in high school. All the girls chased him and he chased them right back."

That gave Paxton pause. Was he like his grandfather?

"But he loved only my grandma." For some reason he thought he should make that clear.

"Now there's a story. Your grandma Martha wouldn't have anything to do with him in high school."

"Why not?"

"Because Martha's daddy was a Baptist preacher and he wasn't letting her date a wild Rebel. That's what they called him—Wild Abe."

Paxton laughed. "I can believe that." He'd heard a lot of stories about his grandma's preacher daddy, but this was a new version. "So how did they finally get together?"

"Well, we all graduated high school. Abe went to work on his dad's ranch and Martha went to work at the courthouse. She still refused to have anything to

do with him. Then one night there was a dance at the
VFW Hall. Her daddy let her go. There's this dance—
I forget what it's called—but all girls hold hands in a
circle and the guys hold hands outside of the girls and
they go around and around as the music plays. When
the music stops, you have to dance with the person in
front of you. That night when the music stopped, Abe
stood right in front of Martha. She tried to turn away,
but he grabbed her arm and started dancing. And they
danced together till the day she died. I don't know what
he said to her to change her mind, but you know Abe
has a lot of charm." She nodded at Paxton. "Like you."

He took a bite of biscuit and mulled over what Miss
Bertie had said. Maybe he was like his grandfather.
Grandpa had been a ladies' man. He'd heard that story
many times. And he'd found a woman to love. A once-
in-a-lifetime love. Maybe there was hope for Paxton,
too.

Very little was said after that. Miss Bertie talked
about the cow, and Remi moved her potatoes around
her plate with a fork.

Miss Bertie tapped her fork against Remi's plate.
"Eat. Put some meat on those bones."

Remi flushed. "Gran, you don't have to keep telling
me I'm thin. I've already been told that." She glanced
at Paxton with a lifted eyebrow.

He did what every cowboy would do when he was
backed into a corner. He winked.

Remi threw a green bean at him. He caught it deftly
and popped it into his mouth. Her jaw dropped opened.

Miss Bertie slapped her hand on the table. "Stop
it. This is the dinner table. Behave yourselves." Both
Remi and Paxton could hardly contain their laughter.

He couldn't remember ever feeling this good inside. It usually required a lot of Jack Daniel's.

Getting to her feet, Miss Bertie said, "Clear the table, Remi, and I'll get the pie."

As Remi carried dishes to the sink, Miss Bertie stepped closer to him and whispered, "So that's the look, huh? I got it now."

"Uh… Um…"

Before he could find a suitable response, a knock sounded at the door. Miss Bertie set the pie on the table and went to answer it.

"What are you doing on my property?" The angry voice had Remi and Paxton rushing into the living room. Ira McCray and Ruger McCray, Remi's uncle and brother, stood just inside the door. In the worn jeans and Western shirts, they had unshaved faces and an unkempt appearance. Remi's brother had always been a little strange, a kind of recluse. He rarely went into town, but occasionally he'd go with his cousins to Rowdy's Beer Joint. He was the type of guy who could wear out a psychiatrist's couch.

Ira pointed a finger at Remi. "Tell her to stop calling Ruger. She only upsets him."

Miss Bertie looked at Ruger. "Did you lose your tongue? Why does your uncle have to speak for you?"

"That's none of your business, you crazy old woman." Ira answered instead of Ruger. "Just tell her to stop calling."

Miss Bertie stepped aside. "Tell her yourself."

Ira stiffened his shoulders and spoke to Remi. "Leave Ruger alone and go back to that whore of a mother of yours."

Remi's eyes narrowed. "I have a right to speak to my

brother and I do not appreciate you calling my mother names."

As Remi spoke, Miss Bertie went into the kitchen and came back with the shotgun in her hands. She pointed it at Ira. "Nobody calls my daughter a whore," she spat. "Say a prayer, Ira, you're about to meet your Maker."

At first Paxton was frozen in disbelief, but he knew Miss Bertie was dead serious. He reached over and grabbed the shotgun as Miss Bertie pulled the trigger. It sounded like a cannon going off in his head. The buckshot fired at the ceiling, and Sheetrock dust rained down on them. Remi screamed, her hands over her mouth. Ira and Ruger stood paralyzed in fear. That was the first thing Paxton noticed. They both were afraid of what Paxton might do with the gun.

He held the power. That was evident by their glazed-over eyes. It was an old-time double-barrel shotgun with two triggers. Both barrels were empty. Miss Bertie had used one shell to get the calves in the trailer and the other she'd fired at the ceiling. But Ira didn't know that.

Paxton pulled the hammer back on an empty barrel. The click echoed loudly through the room. He held the gun in his hand, his finger on the trigger. For years Paxton and his brothers had put up with the McCrays and their attitude, but today Paxton had something to say. And he was going to say it.

"Go ahead fire the gun," Ira said, his throat muscles working overtime. "That's all your family knows how to do. You're a bunch of cold-blooded killers."

Anger simmered through Paxton, but he kept his cool. He still held the power and he felt it all the way to his toes. "Mr. McCray." He looked directly at the man. "You don't mind if I call you that, do you? I was taught to respect my elders."

Ira remained silent.

He pointed the gun toward the ceiling and not directly at the man. "I'm going to tell you the truth about what happened all those years ago. Your brother, Ezra, tried to kill two little boys. They were five and six years old. When my father saw his children lying on the ground bleeding, he jumped over the fence and saw Ezra astride a horse with a rifle in his hands. Ezra lowered the rifle to shoot again, but my dad was faster. He fired first. You know, the fastest draw. Just like in the Old West. That's why the grand jury no billed my father for the death of your brother."

Ira and Ruger still remained silent.

"Now if I lowered this gun and fired at you, that would be cold-blooded murder. But defending yourself and your children is not, Mr. McCray. You've been trying to avenge your brother's death all these years, but you should be trying to come to terms with the fact that your brother had it in him to try to kill two little boys."

"Pull the trigger," Miss Bertie whispered.

Paxton lowered the gun toward the floor. "I'm not a killer and neither was my father, Mr. McCray. And if I were you, I would ease out that door and never come back." He looked at Ruger. "Whatever you do is up to you. Your sister would appreciate a few moments with you, though."

Ira grabbed Ruger by the arm and dragged him through the door.

"No," Remi shouted, running to the door. "Ruger,

please, stay for a few minutes just to talk. We're brother and sister."

"Leave me alone," Ruger muttered lowly, his head bent.

"Ruger," Remi called.

Paxton gently took her arm and pulled her back into the room and closed the door. "He doesn't want to talk to you, Remi. You have to accept that."

She turned on him. "Stop interfering in my life and my business. It doesn't concern you. Please go away and leave me alone." She disappeared through a hallway door.

Sighing deeply, he ran a hand through his hair. Remi was right. This was none of his business and he should've stayed out of it. Her words hurt, but he was a big boy, and it was time for him to go home.

Miss Bertie glared at him. "Why didn't you shoot him?"

"Both barrels were empty."

"Oh, yeah. I forgot to reload."

"And you just don't go around killing people." He held up the gun. "You need to get rid of this thing."

Miss Bertie snorted. "I'll tell you a secret. My eyesight is not what it used to be and if I had pulled the trigger I'd probably have blown a hole in the wall and scared the daylights out of Ira. But then again I might've been dead-on. I really didn't care. No one calls my daughter that."

"Miss Bertie, if you shoot someone, the sheriff is going to arrest you. Is that what you want Remi to see?"

Looking up at the ceiling, she said, "Look what you did." She completely ignored his response.

"You did," he corrected. "You pulled the trigger."

"Oranges and apples." She waved a hand to dismiss the whole thing. "I have to check on my girl."

As Miss Bertie walked to the hall, Paxton noticed a closet. He opened it and put the gun behind some old coats. He hoped she never found it. In the kitchen, he slipped on his jacket and placed his hat on his head. Turning for the back door, Miss Bertie walked in.

"Wait."

He turned back. He wasn't in the mood for more drama.

She pulled a five-dollar bill out of her shirt pocket and handed it to him. "For your gas."

He was tired of playing this little game, too. "Miss Bertie, I don't want your money. It was neighbor helping neighbor."

"That's what Quincy told me when he first started helping me after Edgar died. But I don't want charity. I pay my way."

Paxton took a deep breath. "It's not charity. You cooked a great meal for lunch. That's my payment. I would have eaten a sandwich if I had been home. So consider it paid in full."

She glanced at the table with the pie on it. "Oh, you didn't get dessert."

Paxton held up a hand. "No, that's fine. I really don't want any dessert."

As usual, Miss Bertie wasn't listening to anything he said. She cut a slice of pie and placed it on a plate and then she brought the rest of it to him. "Take this. I saved a piece for Remi." She handed it to him, and he had no option other than to take it. "Don't worry about the plate. Just give it to your mom and she'll bring it back to me."

At a loss for words, he said what anyone would say. "Thank you." Once again, he turned toward the door and stopped. "Miss Bertie, you can call Rusty Scoggins and he'll fix your ceiling and roof. He'll do it at a reasonable price."

"Yeah, I think rain is in the forecast." Miss Bertie eyed him. "You know she's really not mad at you. It's Ruger. She just took it out on you."

"I don't know. It kind of felt like she was mad at me."

"Nah. She didn't mean what she said. I know my girl."

Paxton nodded and went out the door, feeling a sense of relief. And disappointment. Miss Bertie was wrong. He'd somehow managed to hurt Remi once again. But he wasn't going to dwell on it because the gulf between them just got wider.

He placed the pie on the passenger seat and loaded his horse. When he crossed the cattle guard, he knew he wasn't coming back. His good deeds were over. Maybe he was who he was and he should stop trying to be someone else. The ladies' man. The heartthrob. The charmer. That was who he was. Change was just too hard. *Welcome back, Pax.*

REMI SAT UP on the bed and wiped tears away with the backs of her hands. She was tired of crying. She was tired of hurting. She was tired of being angry. And she was tired of not being strong enough to stand up to everyone, especially Ruger. If he didn't want to see her, she should let go, just like Paxton had said.

Her mother had given up a long time ago. In truth, though, her mother really hadn't. She just buried the pain deep inside her, not letting anyone know she was hurting for the loss of her son. But Remi kept holding on, hoping for a connection with her sibling. Today she realized that wasn't going to happen. Ruger was controlled by Ira and that wasn't going to change. She should have learned that after all these years.

Ruger's appearance shocked her. He'd put on weight since the last time she'd seen him, which had been four years. She had called so many times, but he would never answer. His hair and beard were scraggly and he looked as if he hadn't had a bath in days. Clearly, his life was miserable, but he wouldn't let her help him. Nor would he let his mother. It was so sad.

Sadie laid her head in Remi's lap, and Remi stroked her, feeling the calm after a storm. She'd gotten so angry and she had taken her anger out on Paxton. He'd been so nice to her and she would have to apologize.

She found he was easy to talk to and she'd rambled on and on about her life, something she never did. Since the accident, she didn't like to talk about it, but today she couldn't seem to stop. And she'd told him about her deepest, darkest secret—she couldn't have children. She still couldn't believe she'd told him. It didn't matter, though. After today, she would never see him again.

Running her hand over the patchwork quilt on the bed, it reminded her of her messed-up life. Thrown-away pieces of material that Gran had pieced together with patience and love to make something beautiful. Maybe she could find the thread of courage to piece the past and the present together to make a beautiful life. Maybe even make it wonderful. Happy. Somewhere in her she would have to find the strength to face whatever future waited for her.

At times she saw no future without Annie. Once

again, she had to listen to Paxton. She may not get the little girl she loved with all her heart. If that happened, she would have to be strong—stronger than she'd ever been. But she would keep believing until that happened.

She got up and slowly made her way to the kitchen. Gran sat at the table drinking a cup of coffee, staring at a piece of chocolate pie.

"Where's Paxton?" she asked, and looked around the room.

Gran glanced at her. "Where do you think he is?"

"Outside?"

"Sweetie, think. After what you said to him, he didn't feel welcome here."

"Oh, no." Remi covered her mouth in shame. What had she done? "I didn't mean… I was just…"

Gran nodded. "I know, sweetie. You have a lot on your plate right now."

Remi hugged her grandmother and laid her head on her shoulder like she had when she was a kid. She needed that comfort of long ago to sort through her chaotic thoughts. Straightening, she wanted to cry, to give way to tears that always seemed to be there. Not today, though. She was going to stop the waterworks.

She sank into a chair. "I'll apologize as soon as I can."

Her grandmother reached out and caught Remi's hand. "Sweetie, I think you need to figure out what you're feeling for this man. Your emotions are all over the place and you need to give yourself some time to know what you're really feeling. I wish I hadn't asked him to come into the house that night."

Remi frowned. "What are you talking about?"

Gran waved a hand. "Nothing."

"What did you do?"

Gran shifted nervously in her chair and not much made Gran nervous. "You were feeling so down when you got here and I was worried about you. When Paxton arrived, I noticed how handsome he was and I thought he was just the thing to cheer you up. So I asked him to come into the house and give you a compliment to make you feel better."

"What!"

"Now don't get your panties in a twist. I asked, but he refused. I don't know what made him come back. Must be his raising because Kate made sure her boys always respected their elders. And he gave me some bull story about how you'd know the gesture was phony."

"Gran, how could you?" Remi was mortified. As she thought back to that day, she remembered the shock on his face. It was probably the same shock that was on hers at meeting him again in such a way. And he certainly hadn't given her a compliment. Just the opposite. So there was nothing for her to be mad at Gran about, except loving her granddaughter too much. And if Gran hadn't coaxed him into coming into the house, she would never have met him again.

"Because I love you."

"I know." She reached out and touched her grandmother's hand. "I just feel like an ugly duckling or something."

"I don't think Paxton sees you that way."

"You don't." She heard the entreaty in her voice and knew it was time to change the subject.

"Now, don't get your hopes up. Paxton Rebel is a handsome devil and he could break your heart. I wouldn't like to see that because then I would have to hurt him."

A smile tugged at Remi's mouth. "Or I could break his heart."

"Now there's a thought."

Remi looked at her grandmother and thought it was time to broach the subject. "Gran, you really have to stop trying to kill people. I almost had a heart attack when you pulled your shotgun on Uncle Ira."

"Yeah, but did you see his face?"

"Gran, this is not funny. It's serious. You have to put the shotgun up—for good."

"Handsome put it somewhere and I can't find it."

"Smart guy." Remi sat back in the chair. "Where's the rest of the pie?"

"I gave it to Handsome for helping with the cow, but I saved you a piece."

Remi picked up the fork next to the pie. "Ruger doesn't want to see me."

Gran nodded. "If I thought a good slap would knock some sense into him, I'd slap him senseless. But we have to accept it is what it is."

She shoved a chunk of pie into her mouth, tasted its sweetness and thought of Paxton and their conversation. "I told him, Gran."

"Told who what?"

Twirling her fork in the chocolate, she said, "I told Paxton I...I can't have children." The words spoken out loud were just as unacceptable as they were real. Maybe if she kept saying them, they would become as natural as combing her hair.

"My, my. What brought that on? You were very adamant about not telling anyone and your parents and I were—"

"I know." It kind of freaked her out when her parents wanted to talk about it. She had to face the fact that she would never have a child of her own. And she didn't need her parents continually telling her that she was okay. She had to find her own way. Maybe that was why she had told Paxton. She wasn't really sure why; the words had just slipped out.

She told her grandmother about meeting Paxton in Port Aransas. "He was curious as to why I was so weak and kept pushing me, so I told him about Annie and just about everything about my life. It was uncanny, but it was good for me, too."

Her grandmother got up and poured another cup of coffee. "Does this mean you're going to see him again?"

She noticed the stick propped against the wall and thought of Paxton. She had to apologize, but then, she didn't know what that would accomplish except to make her feel better. There was no future for the two of them so she should just stay away from him. The temptation was too great, though, and her conscience needed to be clear.

She got up and reached for the stick and an idea occurred to her. "Gran, do you know of anyone in Horseshoe who could make a top for this, like a cane?"

"Willard Wiznowski owns a blacksmith shop and he can make anything. His wife owns the bakery and they've been here forever. His shop is off Main and not hard to find."

"I think I'll take a trip into Horseshoe."

"Now, you be careful."

"Yes, ma'am."

Paxton had said she needed to use a cane and she had been resisting because of her vanity. But now Paxton had given her the courage to step out of that "poor me" mode and be who she was—someone who was different now, yet the same. He had made her aware she was still very much alive and a woman with needs. All it took was one handsome cowboy.

Chapter Seven

It didn't take Remi long to find the blacksmith shop. She drove through the quaint little country town and glanced at the old brick storefronts. It was like stepping back in time to see a big courthouse sitting in the middle of a square. Two old men sat on benches out front of the building, talking, and people milled around the antiques shops. There was a hive of activity at the bakery. Horseshoe was a place where everyone knew each other and stopped and talked for a few minutes when they met on the street. It felt like home, even though she hadn't lived here since she was a small child.

She stopped at a building that had trucks and trailers parked around it. A man in overalls and a chambray shirt sat on a stool welding a bumper. Sparks flew everywhere and through the hum of the torch she didn't think the man could hear her. She didn't know how to get his attention but she didn't want to get near the sparks. Sadie didn't like them, either, pulling back as Remi moved forward.

The man turned off the torch and removed his helmet. "Can I help you, ma'am?" Before she could respond, he added, "You must be new around here. I don't think we've met."

"I'm Bertie Snipes's granddaughter."

The man stood up and placed a baseball cap on his balding head. She noticed all the burn holes in his overalls and shirt. "You don't say. Your mama took you away when you were just a baby. After the tragedy," he added as an afterthought. "I bet Bertie's happy to have you around."

She held out the stick. "She said you might be able to help me. I'd like to put a top on this, like a cane. Do you think you could do that?"

He ran his hand along the stick. "This is a nice piece of oak and some fine whittling on it."

"Yes. Do you think you could help me?"

"I'd need another piece of oak to finish it."

"The person who made this got it from a branch that had fallen from a tree during a storm. There's still more there."

He peered at her through wire-rimmed glasses. "I didn't know Bertie needed a cane. Why doesn't she just buy one?"

At this point, there were a lot of things Remi could have said or she could've just said nothing. But this was where she became the mature adult and admitted out loud what Paxton had told her.

She took a deep breath. "It's not for my grandmother. It's for me."

Mr. Wiznowski looked her over. "Now, a young thing like you, why would you need a cane?"

Her answer required another deep breath. She'd never said the words out loud and for the first time she knew she had to. "I was in a bad accident a few months ago and my left leg was…severely injured. It hasn't completely healed and I have a problem with balance. The cane helps me with that, as does my dog."

He adjusted his baseball cap. "I'm sorry to hear that. But why don't you just buy a cane?"

She pointed to the stick. "Someone made that especially for me and I want to keep it."

"Well, then, I'll take a look at that tree branch and see if I can make you a top."

Remi smiled. "I'd appreciate that. When do you think you can do it?"

"I'll follow you out to Bertie's and if the wood is good I can start work on it in the morning." He nodded toward the bumper. "I have to finish this trailer hitch today."

"Thank you."

Mr. Wiznowski followed her back to the house and she showed him the branch, which he started at with a chain saw. The noise startled the geese. He finally held up a big piece. "I think this will do it." He took out his pocket knife and scraped away some of the bark. "See, the branch forks here and I'll be able to go up and over and get the top for the cane. I'll put a long screw in the bottom to attach it to the stick and secure it with a couple of staples. It'll take a lot of whittling and it won't be treated or cured wood, but I'll put a sealer on it to protect it."

"Thank you." Remi was happy he could make the cane.

Mr. Wiznowski looked at Remi. "I'll need that." He pointed to the stick in her hand, and she didn't want to let it go. Reluctantly, she handed it to him.

"You'll take good care of it, won't you?"

He opened the door of his truck. "You bet. I'll call

tomorrow if I get it done." He drove toward the corral and the cattle guard.

Slowly, she and Gran walked toward the house.

"You gonna apologize to Handsome?" Gran asked.

"Not tonight. I want the cane to be finished when I do that."

"Why?"

Remi tightened her hand on Sadie's collar. "I want him to know how important it is to me."

"Or how important he is to you," Gran said without missing a beat.

"I don't know, Gran. I'm just feeling my way right now," she admitted.

"Right into a heartache."

Gran could be right and the fact that she was willing to take that risk meant she was much better. She wasn't hiding behind the mask of pain or that mask of disability. She was facing life head-on.

PAXTON SPENT THE rest of the day working with Elias and Jude, repairing a fence that a bull kept breaking. Elias tightened the wires so tight the bull was going to get whiplash if he tried it again. They loaded up their tools and headed toward the barn.

Working with Elias and Jude was an exercise in patience. Elias talked all the time and Jude rarely spoke. He was one of the brothers who'd been shot by Ezra McCray. Ever since that day Jude spoke very little. Their parents had worried about him all the time. But it took a girl to open him up. He met Paige in high school and had no trouble talking to her. They fell in love and they got pregnant. They didn't know what to do because Paige had a full scholarship waiting for her in California. They kept the pregnancy a secret. Paige spoke to a counselor in school and she suggested they give the baby up for adoption, which they did.

But once Paige had the baby and flew away to college, Jude couldn't live with that decision. He talked to his mother and told her about the baby and she helped him get his son back. He raised Zane and they all pitched in. Twelve years later Paige returned and found out Jude had their son. She was furious and there were a lot of fireworks, but in the end they reconnected and today Jude was happy.

Elias was driving the Polaris Ranger and he hit a gopher hole, jarring all of them.

"If you can't drive this thing, let me have the wheel," Jude said, irritated.

"I'm driving, got it?"

"Then watch where you're going," Jude shot back.

But even Jude knew there was no arguing with Elias. He was a law unto himself. He did what he wanted, when he wanted and where he wanted. That was Elias and everyone knew to stay clear when he was angry. Because there was nothing Elias liked better than a good fight.

They made it to the barn without another incident. After storing away the tools, Paxton headed for the bunkhouse. He tried not to think about *her* all afternoon, but she was right there annoying the hell out of him. Why did he even care? That was what he couldn't understand. Walking away was always easy. Why couldn't he get her out of his head?

He sat on the sofa staring at that damn pie. Jericho came out of the bathroom, rubbing his head with a towel. "Where did the pie come from?" he asked.

"It was my payment for helping Miss Bertie."

"Nice. What's for supper? It's your turn to cook."

"Oh, man. I'd forgotten." He got up and opened the refrigerator. "How about hot dogs and chocolate pie?"

"Sounds good."

After dinner, Paxton finished off the last piece of pie and laid his fork in the plate. "Can I ask you a question?"

Rico held up his hands. "No."

"I just want a yes or no. That's it."

Rico pushed back his paper plate. "Okay. I can do that."

Paxton didn't know quite how to word what he was feeling. He rolled it around in his head for a moment. "You've known me for a long time."

"Yep."

"Do you think I'm the kind of man who could love one woman forever? I mean, someone who's not perfect, who needs someone there to help her occasionally."

"You're talking about the granddaughter again, aren't you?"

"There's something there that keeps pulling me toward her and I don't know what it is. I think about her all the time. I don't want to hurt her. I want to be sure about my feelings and I don't know what they are. She makes me so mad sometimes and I know I should just walk away and leave her alone."

"Why don't you?"

"That's my problem. She's living in la-la land and not facing the reality of her situation."

"Which is?"

"She has a lot of recovery ahead of her and she refuses to see she still needs help and she's not completely well."

"And that bothers you?"

Paxton picked up the paper plates and threw them in the trash. "I've never wanted to help anyone in my whole life. Since Dad died, my life has been about me and the rodeo. Of course, I help my mom and my brothers, but I've never had this kind of feeling like I have for Remi. I want her to get better and I want her to be realistic. I can't explain it, but it's eating me up." He wiped his hands on a paper towel. "There's something else. Because of the accident she can't have children."

"That's a biggie."

Paxton leaned against the cabinet. "Yeah. She's trying to adopt her best friend's little girl. Her friend died giving birth. She's planning on being a single mother."

"Wow. That's a lot of problems for a free-living cowboy."

He ran a hand through his hair. "I just want to get her out of my mind."

"You've only known her for a few weeks." Rico got to his feet. "I said I wasn't going to give advice, but you need to take some time to figure out what you're feeling. This girl is going through a lot and is very vulnerable. My advice is to take it slow. And that's my last word on the subject."

"But you didn't say if you thought I could love one woman forever."

"You're the only one who can answer that."

Paxton washed what few dishes there were and decided to stay away from Remi, to give them both time. They barely knew each other. But deep inside he felt as if he'd known her forever. It was the strangest feeling in the world. Yet, it was the best.

REMI WAITED ALL Friday afternoon for Mr. Wiznowski to call. Gran said he was a man of his word and would call when he had it done and for her not to bother him. It was difficult not to call. But she waited. At six o'clock, the call came.

"Do you want me to varnish it?" Mr. Wiznowski asked.

"Yes. I would like that. Thank you."

"Do you want me to file it down so the bottom part is smooth?"

"No. Leave it just like it is." She wanted it just as Paxton had made it and the carving ridges helped her to get a better grip.

"Okay. You can pick it up first thing in the morning. The varnish should be dry by then."

Her heart sank. She wanted to see Paxton tonight, but now she would have to wait until morning. "What time do you open?"

"I'm in the shop about 7:00 a.m."

"I'll be there, and thank you again."

Gran turned from the sink, wiping her hands on a dishtowel. "Willard has it ready?"

"Yes, but I can't get it until the morning."

"That's not too long. It will give you some time to think."

"I know. I know, Gran," she said, walking toward her room. She didn't want to discuss Paxton anymore. She just wanted to explore what she was feeling, and if she got hurt, then it would be her own fault.

She sat on the bed and pulled out her cell to call

Sandy, the nurse on duty where Annie was. They had become fast friends and she knew she could talk to her.

"I know you're on duty and I don't want to keep you, but I'd just like to know how Annie is doing."

"Hi, Remi. We've missed you around here."

"I was asked to leave." That still stung.

"I'm sorry, but that was CPS's decision."

"I know."

"Annie is doing great. She's enjoying all of this attention, so don't worry about her."

"But I do worry. CPS is going to rule in favor of a couple and I'll lose her."

There was silence on the line for a minute. "I'm sorry, Remi. I know how much you love her."

"That doesn't seem to count for much."

"It's not over. CPS is being very thorough and Annie will have the best there is. Just believe that."

After a few more minutes of talking about nonessential things, Remi clicked off. She laid her phone on the bed. The best for Annie was Remi. She wrapped her arms around her waist. Paxton had told her she needed to prepare herself for the fact that she may not get Annie. How did she do that? Not by crying. Not by throwing a temper tantrum. And certainly not by sulking. Annie could have a good home with someone else. She had to start to believe that. It would take a while, though. Maybe a lifetime.

THE NEXT MORNING Paxton dressed in his starched jeans and a white shirt and the gold belt buckle he'd won in Vegas years ago. Tonight he was going to have fun. He was going to make sure he didn't overdo it, but he was getting out and pushing Remi from his head. That was the plan.

First, he had to go to the office and tell the family about the McCrays. He didn't mention it yesterday because he wanted everyone together when he did. He only wanted to say it one time. The office filled up with all the brothers, Mom and Grandpa. Falcon and their mother took their seats behind their desks.

Falcon was the first to speak. "It's Saturday so someone has to feed and check the herds. And we have fifty heifers going to a ranch in Lampasas Monday morning. Someone has to round them up and have them in the pens by Sunday night."

"That's a good job for you," Elias said, and by his tone Paxton knew he was cruising for a fight. "You're getting a little pudgy sitting behind that desk all the time."

Falcon looked up with murder in his eyes. "You want to sit behind this desk, Elias, and make sure this ranch runs at a profit and that we all receive a paycheck every month? Because if you do, I'm willing to hand it over to you."

Falcon's words didn't even faze Elias. "What I'm saying is Jericho and I do all the work around here. It's time someone else stepped up."

Elias was sitting next to Paxton and Paxton leaned over and whispered, "Have you been drinking?"

"No, but if you have a beer, I'll take it."

Egan intervened before any more words could be said. "Jude and I will handle the feeding for the weekend. And we'll get the heifers in the pens by Sunday night."

Falcon looked at Elias again. "Is that okay with you?"

"Hell, yeah."

Their mother joined the conversation. "Son, if you wanted some time off, you should have said something. Take the weekend off. You, too, Jericho."

Jericho held up his hand. "I'm fine. I'll help Egan and Jude."

Their mother stared at Elias. "What's wrong with you this morning?"

"Aw, he fell off a chair last night putting in a light-bulb and hurt his back," Grandpa said.

"I didn't hurt anything," Elias snapped, getting to his feet. "I need to be here for Grandpa."

"No, you don't," Quincy said. "I'll take care of Grandpa. He's at our house most of the time, anyway."

"Y'all are treating me like a little kid." Grandpa got to his feet. "No one needs to take care of me. Now, I'm going to see Jenny and talk to the baby. You know, she reads to the baby and she lets me read, too. That way she can recognize my voice. Did I tell y'all what they're going to name her?"

"About five times this morning," Elias muttered.

Grandpa ignored him. "Martha Kate. Isn't that a beautiful name? My Martha would be so happy." He ambled toward the door and Paxton noticed there was a spring in his step. Naming the baby after their grandmother had given the old man a lift.

Paxton stood. "Wait, Grandpa. I have something to tell the family." He had to tell them about the McCrays because he knew it would be all over town by tomorrow. Ira would make sure of that. "I had an incident with the McCrays yesterday and I wanted you to hear it from me."

His mother was on her feet, worry in her eyes. "What happened?"

"After I finished with the cow at Miss Bertie's, she insisted I stay for lunch. She wouldn't take no for an answer. Ira and Ruger arrived soon after." He told the story as it had happened. "They thought I was going to shoot them, like our father shot Ezra."

He took a deep breath. "Ira said something about cold-blooded murder and I thought it was time to tell him the difference between cold-blooded murder and self-defense. I told them that they needed to acquaint themselves with the truth."

His mother put her arm around his waist. "You handled the situation just right. I'm proud of you."

"Thanks, Mom." He felt like he was ten years old and had helped a little boy who was being bullied in school.

"Good job," Falcon said.

"My boys know how to handle the McCrays." Grandpa nodded. "Just never turn your back on 'em. Now I have to go talk to a baby."

"Just a minute," Falcon called.

"Now what?" Grandpa asked.

"Leah and I have paid off all our medical bills and we've decided to build a house. I talked to Mom and she said it's okay if it's all right with everyone else that I build the house across the road and take the land that goes all the way to the highway. Does anyone have a problem with that?" Falcon looked directly at Elias and Elias shrugged. No one had a problem with the deal.

Grandpa walked out the door and Elias eyed Paxton. "Why are you all dressed up?"

"Cole, Dakota and I are going to a small rodeo down

around Houston to watch Dakota's youngest brother ride his first bull. I told you a week ago."

"I thought you were going to help me get the plumbing hooked up to the well today," Phoenix said.

Paxton turned to his brother. "You never said anything."

"I just thought you'd be here since you're not riding in a rodeo."

"No. I have plans, but I'll help you Sunday afternoon."

"I'll help you," Elias offered.

Phoenix looked at Elias. "Aren't you taking the weekend off?"

"I'll help you first. It won't take long to hook it up."

Their mom patted Elias on the back. "I'm glad my boys get along so well. That's very nice, Elias."

Everyone filed out of the office to go their separate ways. Paxton got in his truck and headed for a fun weekend. As he reached the end of Rebel Road, he glanced both ways. To the left he would travel to US-77 toward Brenham, Texas, to pick up Cole and Dakota, his rodeo buddies. To the right was the road to Miss Bertie's. Part of him wanted to go to the right and apologize for interfering in Remi's life. But the sensible part of him knew he should turn left.

Chapter Eight

Saturday morning Remi was up at 6:00 a.m. She showered and dressed in a black-and-white jogging suit. It was a newer one she liked and she wanted to look nice today. Glancing at the clothes in the closet she had brought with her, she stopped. She could wear jeans, but she felt more comfortable in the jogging pants. They hid all her imperfections.

"Breakfast," Gran called from the kitchen.

"You're all dressed," Gran said as she took a seat at the table.

"Yes. I'm going to pick up the cane as soon as Mr. Wiznowski's opens and then I'm going to see Paxton."

As she dug into her pancakes, Gran sat in a chair and watched her. "Sweetie, slow down. You're not ready for an involvement with a man like Paxton Rebel. And remember Annie? I can't see Handsome wanting to get involved with a woman and a baby. Sorry, but that's the truth."

Remi laid her fork and knife in the plate. "I never forget about Annie. I'm going back to Houston in a few days, so you can stop worrying." She told herself so many times there was no future for her and Paxton, yet she still lingered here in Horseshoe when she should be back home.

"And like magic you'll forget all these feelings you have for him? I'm not so old that I don't remember what it was like being young."

Remi chewed on her lower lip. "Why are you torturing me?"

"I don't want you to get hurt."

She leaned over and smiled at her grandmother. "I'm living and feeling again. Aren't you happy about that?"

Gran got to her feet. "Aw, there's no talking to you. I've got work to do outside."

"Wait. How do I get to Rebel Ranch?"

"You turn right at the end of our road and then it will be the first turn on the left—Rebel Road. You can't miss it. It's a big ranch."

Remi hurried to her bedroom and brushed her hair and put on lipstick. She hadn't bothered with makeup for months, so she didn't today, either. That would be too obvious.

Before Mr. Wiznowski could open the double doors to his shop, Remi was there. The cane was beautiful. He'd done a wonderful job. After paying him and thanking him profusely, she hurried home. It was still too early to show up at Rebel Ranch.

Gran wasn't in the house so Remi poured a cup of coffee and watched the clock. At eight thirty she got up and put her cup in the sink. Sadie trailed after her as she made her way to the back door. Stepping outside, she came to a complete stop. Paxton was coming through the gate. He was here!

All she could do was stare. In tight jeans, a white shirt and a gold belt buckle, Paxton was every girl's dream. His good looks made her heart stop. She was deeply attracted to him and that surprised her. She usually liked guys in suits. But now they seemed effeminate compared to Paxton.

He tipped his hat. "Good morning."

Staring at him, she lost her voice. Clean-shaven and with his carved facial bones, he was masculine and handsome, as Gran called him. He didn't need facial hair to be sexy. *Sexy* was written all over him.

Sadie grunted as she tried to get out of the door Remi was holding, forcing Remi to step farther outside. She held the cane behind her, not wanting him to see it just yet. "I was on my way to see you."

His eyes narrowed. "Why?"

"I wanted to apologize for my behavior the other day. I didn't mean to take my anger out on you. You've been so nice to me and I felt bad about what I said. I didn't mean it. You've helped me more than anyone and I'm grateful for that."

"Ah, Remi. You don't need to apologize. I've interfered in your life too much and I promise not to do it again. You were right."

"But your interfering helped me to open my eyes and see life the way it really is." She took a deep breath. "I may not get Annie, so I'm preparing myself for the worst, just like you said. It isn't easy, though."

She didn't want to get bogged down in feelings that would trigger tears. "Oh, and I was coming to show you this." She held out the cane.

"You bought a cane. I'm impressed."

"No. The bottom part is the stick that you made and I had Mr. Wiznowski put a top on it and the rubber thingy on the bottom."

He ran his hand over it. "Why didn't he file down the ridges?"

"I wanted to leave it the way you made it and it also gives me a better grip to get up."

"You saved the stick?" He seemed confused by her actions.

"Yes. You made me realize I needed one. My vanity kept me from seeing that."

"What about the guys who will be looking at you?"

"I care more about my health and you showed me how stupid it was for me to keep believing that I was well. I'm not, and I have a long way to go."

"Then…"

"What?"

He pointed to her outfit. "Why do you hide your body in frumpy clothes? You're a beautiful woman. You don't need to hide a thing."

"I…" She wasn't sure how to respond so she didn't. She'd been tempted to wear jeans and now she wondered why she didn't. Everyone knew she'd been in an accident and she wasn't the same anymore. Paxton had a way of making her see things more clearly.

He held up a hand. "Forget I said that. I'm sticking my nose in again where it doesn't belong."

"No, you're right. I guess I'm hoping that one day I'll take off my clothes at night and my leg will be the way it was before the accident. You know that dream-world I live in."

"Remi." A longing filled his voice and she felt it all the way to her heart.

They stared at each other for several seconds. Finally, Paxton said, "I'm on my way to a rodeo and I don't know what I'm doing here. I just couldn't leave things the way they were between us. I wanted to say I'm sorry. Now—" he looked directly into her eyes

"—there's something happening between us. I don't know what it is, but I can't seem to stay away from you."

He took her breath away and she had trouble finding words again. She didn't expect him to be so honest. "I feel the same way about you and it scares me. My life is in Houston and your life is on the rodeo circuit. I have a lot of healing to do and then there's Annie. I keep asking myself why I'm so attracted to you."

"Yeah. There's that." He stepped closer to her and brushed her hair behind her ear with a hand that was so gentle she caught her breath. A tangy masculine scent stirred her senses even more.

"Will...will there be girls at this rodeo?"

"Lots of girls," he whispered, his eyes on her lips.

"Oh."

A loud banging interrupted them. Paxton's eyes left hers and she felt bereaved. "Where's your grandmother?"

"She said she had something to do."

The banging continued.

"I better check," he said, and went down the steps to the side of the house. Remi followed more slowly.

Her grandmother had a big ladder and she was trying to place it against the house, but she wasn't having any luck.

"What are you doing?" Paxton asked.

"I have to fix this roof. It's supposed to rain tonight." She pointed to the ground where a big piece of plastic lay. "I'm gonna put that over the holes and tack it down so my ceiling won't get wet."

Paxton took the ladder from her. "You're not climbing this ladder. Didn't you call Rusty?"

"Yeah. He wanted two hundred and fifty dollars to fix my roof. I can't afford that."

Paxton sighed. "Did that include the inside?"

"Yes, and he said I needed to paint the living room. I told him I wasn't and to get out of my house."

Paxton dropped the ladder on the side of the house. "Okay, Miss Bertie, this is what we're going to do. I'm going home to change my clothes and then I'm going to buy the shingles and tar paper and whatever I need to do this job. I'm going to charge everything to you and you're going to pay for it."

"Now listen here. I told you I don't like men telling me what to do."

"I'm telling you." Paxton's voice was strong, and even Gran could see he wasn't going to bend on this.

"Paxton, no," Remi said. "I'll call this Rusty guy and you can go on to the rodeo. I'm sure he'll come back and fix it if I pay him."

Paxton looked at her. "He doesn't work on weekends. It's okay. I'll do it."

"But you have plans."

He winked at her. "Now I have other plans." He walked past her with a glint in his eyes and she felt giddy. He turned back. "Don't let your grandmother use that ladder."

Remi glared at her grandmother. "How could you, Gran? You could have broken your neck on the roof. And when did that guy come by? I never saw him."

"He came while you were at the blacksmith shop. I'm not paying that much money to fix this roof."

Remi shook her head. "I think I'll call Mom and let her talk to you." Remi knew that was a sore subject.

Her mother was always trying to get Gran to move to Houston with them.

Gran shook her finger in Remi's face. "Don't you dare. I'm going to the house to fix lunch. If Handsome is going to be here, I have to have a good meal."

There was no use talking to Gran. She lived by her own rules and she was never going to break them. Paxton had made her back down and that was something to see. Now he was staying. He was staying! A slow smile spread across her face.

Could it be because of her?

PAXTON DROVE TO the bunkhouse and changed into old jeans and a T-shirt. Slamming a foot into worn boots, he wondered what he was doing. He should be half-way to Houston by now instead of dealing with a crazy old lady. But then there was Remi. She'd made a cane from that stick and he couldn't get that out of his head. It was symbolic in some way, but he couldn't figure it out just yet.

He'd wanted a change in his life and he'd got more than he'd bargained for. But he was going to be the man his dad had wanted him to be and he knew that meant not letting a little old lady climb a ladder to put plastic on her roof. Maybe he had some of those do-gooder genes, after all.

Sitting on the bed, he pulled out his phone and called Cole.

"Hey," Cole responded. "What time are you getting here?"

"Sorry, buddy, but I can't make the rodeo."

"Why not? We had this planned for weeks. Oh, you

got family stuff going on, huh?" Cole said before Paxton could answer.

"Kind of."

"Okay. I'll see you on Friday, then. I'll be at your place about eight in the morning."

"Don't be late." They were going to a rodeo in Glen Rose, Texas. After that, it would be rodeo time for the next few months.

Over an hour later he was back at Miss Bertie's with all the supplies. He carried the paint, brushes, rollers and pans in first. The smell of Miss Bertie's kitchen was heavenly. She was cooking something delicious and if he had to guess he'd say peach cobbler. Remi wasn't in the kitchen and Miss Bertie followed him into the living room.

"What's all that? What did it cost?" She was yapping faster than a chirping bird.

He set the supplies on the floor. "It's paint and rollers to paint this room after I put putty in the holes and spackle it."

"I told you I'm not painting this room." Her old green eyes dared him to defy her.

"Then you can watch me." He stood up straight, his hands on his hips.

"Remi was right. You're sticking your nose in where it doesn't belong. This is my house and I don't want to paint it."

"Gran!"

Remi stood in the doorway in jeans and a green knit top. She'd changed her clothes. For him. She looked gorgeous, but he couldn't say that because she would think it was phony. The green of her top brought out the green of her eyes, and he was spellbound.

Gran turned to her. "Look at you. My old Remi's back."

"Why don't you want to paint this room?" Remi asked, not letting her grandmother sidetrack her. "It hasn't been painted in years. A new coat of paint would do wonders for it."

"Well?" Paxton looked at the old woman for an answer.

She ran her hands down her apron. "I don't want to paint it because I'd have to take down the Elvis poster. It's vintage and it's been there so long I'm afraid it'll fall to pieces if I move it."

Good heavens! What was it with Elvis?

"Do you have some small paintbrushes?" he asked.

"I did a craft thing at the senior citizen center a few years ago. I think I have some brushes in my bedroom. I'll go look."

Paxton focused on Remi. "Well, well, well, don't you look great?"

She looked down at her jeans. "I thought my injured leg would be noticeable in these, but it isn't. It's completely straight."

Paxton kept staring at her. "Yes, it is. You even have hips."

She tilted her head, her eyes sparkling. "Are you flirting with me again?"

"Whatever works," he said with a smile in his voice.

Miss Bertie came back, preventing further conversation. She held several small paintbrushes in her hands. "Will these work?"

He took one from her. "Yes. I'll use this very carefully to paint around the Elvis poster and promise not to get any on it. Will that suit you?"

She nodded. "But what are you going to charge me for doing all this?"

"I don't know. We'll discuss it later."

"We'll discuss it now," Miss Bertie shot back.

Paxton thought for a minute. He didn't want a dime, but he didn't know how to convince Miss Bertie of that. "Is that peach cobbler cooking in the oven?"

"It sure is."

"It's my favorite dessert, so if you'll cook me one every now and then, we'll be even."

She held out her hand. "Deal."

He shook it and was amazed at her strength. After that he moved all of the furniture to the center of the room. Remi took all the Elvis memorabilia off the walls, and then she removed all the family photos and laid them on the sofa. Paxton stopped mixing spackle to stare at a young Remi. Her hair was long, very long. He saw her from a baby to a teenager to an adult and her hair had always been long. Obviously, it had been cut while she was ill and in the hospital. The photos showed just how beautiful she was, but in his gut he knew she didn't think she was, even before the accident.

After he fixed the holes, Miss Bertie shouted, "It's time for lunch."

She'd prepared chicken fried steak and all the trimmings. Afterward, he refused peach cobbler and said he would eat it later when he was through. Miss Bertie didn't object.

Before going outside to work on the roof, he painted around the Elvis poster very carefully and wondered how an old lady could be so obsessed with the man. Then it hit him. His mother might be, too, but he never saw any Elvis memorabilia around the house.

He left the ladies painting and backed his truck to the side of Miss Bertie's house. Then he climbed the ladder and tore off the damaged roof. He was almost finished when Remi came out with a glass of iced tea. The temperature was mild, but a cold front with rain was expected, and Paxton wanted to finish the roof before that happened.

"Would you like something to drink?" She had a handkerchief tied around her head and one of her grandmother's baggy shirts to cover her blouse, but she was still beautiful to him.

He went down the ladder and sat on a rung, taking the tea glass from her hand. "Thanks." He nodded toward her attire. "How's the painting going?"

"We're almost finished. And we're following orders and waiting for you to do the ceiling."

"I have a few more shingles to nail on and then I'll be in."

She looked at him and he got lost in the green of her eyes. "Thank you for doing this."

"My pleasure, ma'am."

"Sometimes your words have a double meaning."

With a finger he wiped paint from her cheek. "Yes, ma'am."

She turned around and walked toward the house, using the cane, with Sadie.

He thought once again about what he was doing here, but it made him feel good inside. It made him feel good about himself. Other than that, he couldn't explain it. He was tired of trying to figure it out. He was just going to go with the moment and let his heart work out the rest.

THEY HAD A busy afternoon. Remi helped Paxton pick up the scrap from the roof that had missed the back of his truck. Then he hauled it off to Gran's brush pile. After the walls were dry, Paxton moved all the furniture back in place, and the Elvis poster was intact and hadn't been moved.

Remi looked around the room. "It's so nice, isn't it, Gran? Gives it a fresh look."

"Yeah, yeah. Who wants peach cobbler?"

Remi and Paxton took theirs outside to the front porch and sat in the swing. Paxton propped his legs on the porch railing and devoured the peach cobbler. "You really like it?"

"Yes, ma'am."

She slapped his arm. "Stop calling me that."

"Yes—" He laughed. "Sorry, it's just ingrained in all of us. We were taught to say 'yes, ma'am' and 'no, sir' at an early age. My parents were big on respect."

Thunder rumbled across the sky, and Sadie barked. Paxton looked out at the darkening sky. "I got that roof on just in time." As the last word left his mouth, rain peppered the grass and the porch. He took her plate. "I'll take these inside. Don't move."

She settled back in the swing, rocking back and forth, as the rain continued to fall. It was soothing. Paxton came back with an afghan and handed it to her.

"It's getting chilly out here." He nodded toward the house. "Your grandmother is asleep in her chair."

"She's had a long day."

He looped the afghan over her shoulders. It was the end of February and the cold front was moving through. Paxton sat beside her again, his long legs stretched out in front of him.

"Are you tired?" she asked.

"Nah. I'm used to work." It was unusual to find a

man who thrived in everything he did. She might be wearing rose-colored glasses, too.

They were silent for a while as they listened to the rain. "I'm sorry you missed the rodeo."

"Haven't you heard the saying 'there's always another rodeo'?"

"Were you going to ride?"

"No. We decided to only ride in the Fort Worth Livestock Show and Rodeo this year. My friends and I were just checking out the competition. It was just a fun weekend."

Lightning zigzagged across the sky and Remi jumped. Paxton put his arm around her. "Are you afraid of lightning?"

"A little." She snuggled into his side, feeling comfortable. He wrapped the afghan around them as the temperature continued to drop. They sat there watching the rain as the daylight slowly ebbed into darkness. She should turn on the porch light, but she was too comfortable to move.

She played with a button on his shirt. "You like blondes?"

"Most of the time."

"I'm not blond."

"I noticed."

"So why are we sitting here like lovers?"

His hand stroked the back of her neck. "I don't know. When I looked into your eyes on the beach in Port Aransas, I felt a connection like I've never felt before. Your eyes were sad, lonely and afraid, and somehow I identified with that."

"Why? You're none of those things."

"I come from a big family and there's always someone around, but when I was growing up I felt left out of things. Falcon and Quincy were buddies and always together. Egan was a loner and stayed to himself. Elias was much the same, but Elias is very outspoken where Egan is reserved. Jude and Phoenix were born in the same year so they were close. I was in the middle and at times I felt lonely. I can't explain it, but I did. Then I lost my dad and my whole world unraveled."

She patted his chest. "I'm so sorry about that."

"Why? You had nothing to do with it."

"But I can feel your pain when you talk about him."

"Yeah… Remi, I don't know why we're attracted to each other, but I want you to know up front that I'm not the staying kind. Love 'em and leave 'em, that's me."

"Why do you want me to think that you're bad?"

"Maybe it's better that way."

She tilted her head back. "Kiss me."

He kissed her forehead, a touch of warmth radiated through her. But it wasn't what she wanted. "My grand-mother kisses me that way."

"Remi…"

Boldly, she touched her lips to his. They were cool and unresponsive, but she felt the warmth simmering in him. Suddenly, his lips took hers and the heat ignited every sense in her body. She was being kissed by a man who knew how to kiss. And had kissed many women. That didn't bother her. She was the woman he was kissing now.

She wrapped her arms around his neck and lost herself in the sweet sensation of feeling like a woman again. Totally in control, he kissed her deeply, their tongues doing a dance that totally enraptured her. She just wanted it to go on. But they had to come up for air.

He rested his forehead against hers. "Let's don't ask questions. Let's just enjoy what we're feeling. Okay?"

"Okay," she murmured, and rested her head on his shoulder as the night wrapped around them. The rain continued to pepper the house and it lulled them into a feeling of contentment. Just the two of them. Without problems. Without families. Without commitments.

If only they could stay this way. The real world was waiting beyond the darkness, but she had this moment with him and it was enough for now.

Chapter Nine

Since Paxton was leaving on Friday and Remi was going back to Houston soon, they agreed to spend the next few days together, or at least the evenings. Paxton had to work during the day, but as soon as he was done he showered and headed for Remi's. He didn't question what he was doing. He just wanted to be with her.

On Sunday afternoon he took her to Phoenix's to meet Rosie, her cousin. There was a lot of laughter, tears, hugs and kisses. The two couldn't stop talking. While Rosie and their son, Jake, showed Remi the new house, Phoenix pulled Paxton aside.

"She walks with a cane."

Paxton frowned. "So? Do you have a problem with that?"

"It's like what's wrong with this picture. Paxton Rebel is dating a woman who uses a cane. The last woman you were head over heels in love with looked like a model from Victoria's Secret. She was hot. All your women have been hot. So yes, I'm wondering what's going on with you. Remi is real, like the girl next door, and you could hurt her badly."

"Okay. She's not the kind of woman I usually date,

but I like her and she makes me feel good about myself. I just like being around her."

"So now you need someone to cheer you up?"

Paxton placed his hands on his hips, trying not to lash out at his brother. He had a right to question what Paxton was doing. Paxton had questioned it himself. But it was his business and he didn't like his brother sticking his nose in.

He looked directly at his brother. "You don't think I can change?"

"Not like this." Phoenix snapped his fingers. "On New Year's Eve, which was two months ago, you and Elias were out with women you don't even remember. That's you. The party guy. The one I know."

"I'm not that guy anymore," he stated firmly.

Phoenix studied him. "You seem different. More serious. How did that happen?"

Paxton pointed toward the house. "She makes me want to be a better person, a better man. I would never hurt her."

Phoenix shook his hand. "Does Mom know about this? Falling for a McCray is a big deal for a Rebel and I'm giving you a warning. You tell Mom first."

"She already knows."

"What!"

"I told her because I didn't want to go through what you did. Naturally, she doesn't like it, but she knows Remi had nothing to do with Dad's death or the shooting. She also gave me a warning. I seem to be getting a lot of those these days." He poked a finger into Phoenix's chest. "Now who's more grown up?"

Jake darted out of the house. "Uncle Pax, Uncle Pax." The boy held up his arms for Paxton to take hir swung his nephew into the air and giggles erupted, filling the afternoon with happy vibes. A smile tugged at the corners of his mouth and his eyes met Remi's. She was standing on the sidewalk, watching him.

There was no doubt in his mind that he felt something for her, but on the way home Phoenix's doubts nagged at him. An old truck was parked in front of Miss Bertie's house. Paxton knew it was Ruger's.

While he was searching for words, she spoke up. "You're very quiet. Did Phoenix say something to you while we were there?"

He waited too long to respond and she knew that Phoenix had. "What did he say?"

"Nothing. Just brother talk."

He drove the truck to the back, got out and hurried around to the passenger side to help Remi. But she was already standing on the ground, her face creased into a frown. "Phoenix had questions about me, didn't he?"

"Remi…"

"I'm not the type of girl you usually date."

"Will you stop it? It has nothing to do with you. It's about me. Phoenix doesn't want me to hurt you. That's it. We talked about this ourselves. I don't see why you're so upset."

"I think we should stop seeing each other," she said quietly, and turned toward the house.

His stomach knotted into a ball, but he hurried after her. "Remi, that was Ruger's truck in front of the house."

She frowned at him. "Why didn't you tell me?" She didn't wait for an answer as she made her way inside.

Paxton had two choices. He could leave or stay in case Remi or Miss Bertie needed help. He did the latter.

Ruger and his grandmother stood in the kitchen.

Miss Bertie was all smiles. Ruger's clothes were clean and it looked as if he'd cut his hair.

"Look who came for a visit," Miss Bertie said, patting Ruger on the shoulder.

"What are you doing here?" Remi asked.

"I didn't mean to hurt you. Uncle Ira gets upset when you call and I'd rather not deal with the hassle."

"But you're here. What's he going to say about that?"

Ruger shrugged. "Nothing good. I've been thinking about what you—" he glanced at Paxton "—said about the shooting. You got it all wrong. Uncle Ira said your brothers fell off the horse and injured themselves. My father was a good man. He wouldn't shoot a kid."

"A good man!" Miss Bertie's eyes almost bugged out.

"Ruger." Remi moved closer to him. "Mom told me a lot about what happened back then." She reached around and lifted Ruger's shirt.

Miss Bertie gasped.

"Did a good man put those marks on your back? Mom said they were from his belt. You were always trying to protect her and then you'd get the beating. And there were a lot of times she had to pull him off you because you'd done some silly little thing like forget your coat at school. He wasn't a good man, Ruger. That's what Uncle Ira wants you to believe."

Ruger paled and seemed speechless.

"Jude has a scar on his forehead where a bullet grazed him," Paxton said. "It was confirmed at the hospital that he'd been shot at. My brothers didn't fall off the horse. Your father tried to kill them. It's public record. You can read it down at the courthouse."

Ruger shook his head. "I don't know. Uncle Ira…"

Remi put her arms around her brother and hugged him. "Uncle Ira lied."

"I'm so confused. I have to go." Ruger hurried toward the front door, but Miss Bertie caught up with him and hugged him, too.

"You're always welcome here."

After Ruger left, Paxton said, "I have to go, too. Can we talk first?"

She looked at him, her eyes sad, much as they had been the day he'd met her. So many emotions churned inside him, but above everything he wanted things to be right between them.

"No." She shook her head. "We don't need to talk. I overreacted. I was just disappointed that your brother thought I wasn't good enough for you."

"Aw, Remi." He moved closer to her. "It was just the opposite. He doesn't think I'm good enough for you. Phoenix and I have traveled the circuit for a lot of years and lived a rather rough life on the road. There were many women and many one-night stands. He doesn't think you're the type of girl for a one-night stand. And he's right."

"I'm not that naive, Paxton."

"In some ways, you are."

She pointed a finger at him. "You don't know the type of life I've led. I've been around, too."

He bit her finger. "You're lying."

"If you do that again, I'm going to smack you."

"Bite me." He smiled into her angry eyes.

She took a couple steps forward and stood on her tiptoes to bite his chin. Soft and lightly as if she didn't want to hurt him. He laughed.

"What? You said to bite you." She cocked her head to

the side as if she was trying to measure him up and then she did something unexpected. She wrapped her arms around his waist and rested against him. He melted like ice on a hot day. He'd never met anyone quite like her.

"That better be a goodbye hug," Miss Bertie said as she came into the kitchen.

"It is, Gran." Remi turned to her grandmother. "Can you believe Ruger came over?"

Miss Bertie glanced at Paxton. "I think it has something to do with Handsome here. Ruger finally heard the story in a way that he could understand. It's going to take him a while to believe the truth."

"I have to go," Paxton said, knowing it was time for him to leave. The women needed some time alone. But he hesitated. He wasn't clear about his and Remi's situation.

Remi smiled at him. "I'll see you tomorrow night?"

"You bet." That was all he needed to hear. She wanted to see him again. He walked out the door feeling good about the day and about Remi.

THE REST OF the week went smoothly, but they both were very aware that Thursday would be goodbye. Paxton would leave for the rodeo circuit and Remi would return to Houston.

They spent most evenings on the porch swing, necking like teenagers. Paxton always stopped when things got heated. He wanted her, but he wasn't really sure if Remi was ready for an intimate relationship, especially since they would be parting ways on Thursday. That wasn't like him at all. He always took what he wanted. But Remi was someone special and he wanted their first time to be special. The times with her made him feel young and alive again, full of vim and vigor. He took a lot of cold showers. Rico laughed at him. He never felt happier in his whole life.

Thursday night arrived faster than he wanted. He and Remi stood outside by his truck in the moonlight, holding on tight. He just wanted to go on kissing her forever. She rested her forehead on his chest. A frog croaked from the pond and the *whoo whoo* of an owl broke into the silence of their feelings. A peaceful country evening, but inside Paxton was hurting.

"I'll miss you," she murmured.

"Me, too." He didn't want this to be goodbye.

They were silent for a moment as Paxton leaned against his truck, holding her. He never dreamed that leaving would be this hard.

"Good luck on the circuit," she whispered into his chest.

"Thanks. And good luck with therapy and Annie. I hope it all works out for you."

"I'm prepared now for whatever happens. Thanks to you." She patted his chest, her hand lingering longer than necessary. She looked up at him and even though it was dark he could see her green eyes in the moonlight. Not clearly, but enough.

Stepping away from him, she said, "Take care of yourself. I'll never forget you."

She walked away with Sadie before he could find words. His throat was dry, yet his hands were clammy. He forced himself to get in his truck and drive away.

He didn't know a lot about change, but he knew one thing—whatever had happened in the last few weeks had turned him into a different person. He wasn't ever going to be that playboy again. Or the ladies' man. He wanted more and he was so afraid he'd just left it behind.

REMI WAS UP early the next morning and had her car packed by eight o'clock. She and Gran managed to get her stationary bicycle in the back of her SUV. She tried not to think about Paxton, but he was right there with every breath she took. It would take a while to forget him. If ever.

She lingered, talking to Gran and hoping Ruger would come by. She wanted to say goodbye.

"So you said goodbye to Handsome?"

Remi placed the last of her things in a suitcase. "Yes. I'll never see him again, but I'll remember him. I'm going to see my lawyer as soon as I get back to Houston and let her know how much I've improved. I've already called my therapist/trainer and he's scheduled me for appointments. My focus now is totally on Annie."

A knock sounded at the front door, interrupting them. Gran jumped up to open the door. Ruger walked in and Remi hugged him. "I'm so glad you came back."

"Gran said you were leaving today and I wanted to see you." He was clean-shaven once again and he was looking more like the old Ruger. "I wanted to tell you not to call my cell. Uncle Ira checks it all the time. I'll come see Gran and I'll call you from here."

"Ruger, why don't you just move away? You can live here with Gran."

"I don't want to talk about it," he replied sharply.

She hugged him again. "We love you and Mom does, too."

"I have a lot of thinking to do."

Remi didn't push him. The fact that he was here

was a big step forward. She said goodbye and got in her car and drove away. She hated to leave Gran, but she knew her grandmother was very strong and had a lot of friends in Horseshoe who would look out for her, especially the Rebels.

She made it to her parents' house in time for lunch. She was surprised to see her dad's car in the garage. He usually didn't have time to come home during the lunch hour. She paused for a moment to gaze at the two-story colonial-style home she had grown up in. There was a pool in the backyard and she'd had every luxury there was. She'd never wanted for anything. But Horseshoe, Texas, was always at the back of her mind. Even though she was a baby when the tragedy had happened, she knew it had affected everyone in her family.

In the kitchen, her mom and dad were eating. "Hey, hey, I'm home."

Her mother jumped up to hug her. "Look at you. You're walking with a cane. You resisted that when the doctors mentioned it." Everyone said she looked like her mother, but she never thought so. Her mother was beautiful and Remi paled in comparison. Her mother was taller and blonde and outgoing, getting involved with a lot of charities and events at the hospital.

"A handsome cowboy changed my mind."

"What's this?" Her dad gave her a bear hug. Of medium height with graying brown hair, her dad was a kind and caring man. So many times she'd cried on his shoulder when things went wrong in her life. She grew up thinking he could fix everything. She couldn't imagine what it would have been like to be raised by Ezra McCray.

She slid into a chair. In her late teens she'd been reluctant to share her life with her parents because they were so protective. But the accident, ironically, had improved their relationship. Her parents now listened instead of ordering her not to do something and she felt comfortable sharing with them. She told them about Paxton.

They glanced at each other, but neither said a word. "You don't have to worry. I'm not seeing him again. He's back on the rodeo circuit."

"Sweetheart." Her mother hugged her from behind. "Did it bother you that he was part of the Rebel family?"

"At first it did. But then I got to know him and I could see he was a very nice man."

"You seem to like this young man a lot." Her dad took a seat, his eyes on her.

"I do," she admitted. "But, you know, he's a Rebel and I'm a McCray. And we live very different lives. Plus, there's my health. There are just so many things standing in our way. So, you don't have to worry. I'm going to concentrate on my therapy and Annie."

She couldn't leave without letting her mother know there was a change in her brother. She told her the whole story about Ira and Ruger and the shooting, and Ruger coming back.

"Ruger actually listened to Paxton Rebel?" her mother asked, excitement in her voice.

"Yes. He finally heard the story from someone other than Uncle Ira. He's confused right now. We just have to wait."

"I'm beginning to like this cowboy of yours."

Remi was happy about that. But she knew in her heart there was no future for them.

PAXTON WAS UP early and had his truck and travel trailer packed and ready to go. In the next few days he would try to put Remi out of his mind because rodeo now came first.

Then he went over to see Quincy and Jenny because he probably wouldn't be home for the birth of their child and he wanted to wish them the best. Next he went to the office. Everyone had already left, except his mom, who was at her desk. He had to say goodbye to his mom. It was something he and Phoenix had always done.

Her eyes lit up when she saw him. "I thought you'd forgotten." She came around the desk and hugged him and he was reminded once again how strong his mother was, holding them all together with her love and strength. They had disappointed her at times, but she always forgave them.

"I'll see you in a couple weeks. I'll call when I'm on the way home."

"Son?"

He looked back. "Bertie said you and Remi were getting really serious."

He was hoping to avoid the subject. "Yeah. We like each other. We seem to have a connection, but she's going back to Houston and I'm hitting the circuit. I probably won't see her again." The thought made his stomach ache.

"Do you want to?"

More than anything on this earth.

"I'll let you know when I get back. Once I'm away from her and back in my old lifestyle maybe all these—" he put his hand over his heart "—feelings will disappear."

"It doesn't work that way, son."

He looked at her. "You're very calm about this."

"I learned my lesson with Phoenix. You can't stop love. I wish she wasn't a McCray, but I can't change that."

"Ah, Mom." He put an arm around her shoulders. "I'm sorry if all this is hurting you."

She patted his face. "I want what I want for all my sons. I want you to be happy."

He nodded and went out the door. Cole and Dakota arrived and they were off for a season of rodeoing. They took Paxton's truck because it had a hitch for the travel trailer and he liked to drive.

Cole had the radio turned up loud so there wasn't much talking except for Dakota laughing that his brother had given up bull riding after one ride. Dakota settled back and went to sleep. Another typical day in rodeo life. Once they arrived in Glen Rose, they parked the trailer and hooked up to electricity. Then they went to sign in and get their numbers. After that, they had a little time to look around and rest before the rodeo tonight. Cole and Dakota were off with their friends. Paxton didn't care to go and sat on the stoop of the trailer and wondered if Remi had made it back to Houston. He had to stop thinking about her. He got up and went inside to work on his bull rope. Everything had to be just right, the way he wanted. A lot of cowboys bought their ropes, but Jude had helped Phoenix and Paxton make their own. The braided rope had to be tight and secure and the handle had to be big enough to just hold his right hand, giving him enough space to hold on for eight seconds. Keeping the rope clean was a big deal. He used a wire brush and glycerin soap. He never forgot to clean his bull rope before storing it away.

With this duffel bag in his hand, he walked over to the arena. It was coming alive as people filled the stands and the smell of popcorn and hot dogs made him realize he hadn't eaten lunch. Country music played in the background and the smell of manure and bulls perfumed the air. It was rodeo time.

He wore his red shirt, like always. It was a trademark for him—his lucky charm. He found when he wore the red shirt he always made the eight-second ride. He shook hands with old friends that had been around the circuit. Suddenly someone slapped him on the back.

He turned around and the young boy held out his hand. "You're Paxton Rebel. I've watched you ride for years. I've learned from you and this year I'm going to kick your butt." Barron Flynn stood in front of him as arrogant as any twenty-year-old could be. He'd made a name for himself riding some tough bulls and he was working his way toward the title.

"If you've learned anything from me, you know I don't brag. Good luck." He walked away with his duffel bag.

"Hey," Barron called after him. "I was only joking."

Usually he would've handled that differently, but he wasn't in a joking mood. He had lost the Paxton who had joked and laughed and fooled around. He didn't want to be that drunk cowboy who was just out for a good time. And that was the way he had been at most rodeos. This year it was for real. Just like Remi.

The cowboys stood on the deck, waiting for their turn. Cole got bucked off and Dakota scored an eighty-four. Barron was ahead of Paxton, who was the last cowboy to ride. Barron had drawn War Horse. The bull was rank and it would take some experience to ride him.

Paxton leaned on the railing, watching. War Horse flew into the arena bucking and turning, and still Barron stayed on. He scored an eighty-six, the highest of the night. A knot formed in Paxton's stomach as he climbed the rails to ride Ornery Cuss. He had never ridden the bull, but he'd studied him in videos.

Carefully, he slid onto the bull's back. Cole and Dakota helped him to adjust the bull rope. Dakota handed him a lump of rosin and he broke it in his gloved right hand and worked it into the handle of the bull rope and into the glove for a tight grip.

"Ready?" Cole asked.

At this point, Paxton shut everything out. The voices, the noise, the crowd, everything. Even Remi. He raised his left hand in the air and nodded. The gate flung open and Ornery Cuss burst into the arena, kicking out with his back legs and flinging his head in the air, doing everything he could to dislodge his rider. But Paxton held on and when the buzzer went off, he jumped off and ran for safety. He climbed over the railing and waited for the score. The knot in his stomach got bigger. When eighty-seven popped up, he raised a fist in the air. Beating the young kid was a good feeling. But he'd have to beat him tomorrow night, too, to win the rodeo.

The first night came to an end and the cowboys packed up their gear. Cole came charging toward him almost out of breath. "Hey, there's some girls outside and they want to know if we want to party tonight."

"I'm in," Dakota said, as did several other cowboys.

Cole looked at him. "How about you?"

He picked up his duffel bag. "Not tonight. I'm going back to the trailer."

"What! The girls asked for you. You have to go." Cole was persistent.

Paxton shook his head. "Not interested."

Cole placed his hands on his hips. "There's something wrong with you. You're not the old Paxton."

Paxton smiled. "Exactly." He walked away, leaving stunned faces behind him.

He went to the trailer, took a shower and lay on his bed. The trailer was small, but good enough for what they needed for the circuit. It had one bedroom, a small kitchen, a bath and a living area. The sofa made into a bed and that was where Cole and Dakota slept.

Stuffing pillows behind his head, he heard his phone. He leaped for his jeans, looped over a chair, and found it. It was his mother. His heart sank. He'd hoped it would be Remi.

"Hi, Mom."

"I know it's late, but I wanted to let you know Jenny had the baby. A six-pound beautiful Martha Kate. She looks just like Jenny."

"Is everyone okay?"

"Jenny and baby are fine. Quincy is happier than I've ever seen him in his whole life. He won't let go of the baby. He carries her around the room, talking to her. Everyone's here. We miss you. Elias is trying to get Grandpa to go home and I'm sure Grandpa will cause a scene. He doesn't want to leave."

Typical Rebel family drama.

"Tell them I said congratulations and I can't wait to see the new addition to the family."

He clicked off and sat propped up in bed with the phone in his hand. He missed the family, too. For the first time since he'd started riding the circuit, he missed being home. It was a sobering thought.

To keep from feeling lonely, he got up and went in the kitchen and ate Oreos and a glass of milk. He held up his glass. "Here's to you, Quincy and Jenny. Glad you're happy."

Would he ever find the kind of happiness his brothers had? Of course his thoughts turned to Remi. He told himself they were wrong for each other. She was a McCray. She had serious problems to overcome, and yet he couldn't stop thinking about her.

After washing the glass, he went back to bed, but he couldn't sleep. He stuffed pillows behind his back and reached for his phone. He could call her, but they'd agreed to end the relationship. As he stared at his phone, a picture popped up—a picture of the baby. It was from Quincy.

Paxton texted him back, congratulating him on his new daughter. Happiness and love. What was it all about? Suddenly he knew. The ache inside him wouldn't go away until he talked to her. Remi was his happiness. She'd given him her phone number, and he touched her name on his cell. He waited and waited.

REMI RODE HER stationary bicycle, trying to get her miles in for the day. Her phone pinged and she leaned over to look at it on the bed. *Paxton.* Why was he calling? It was hard enough to let go. If she heard his voice, she would weaken.

Don't answer. Don't answer. Don't answer.

But… She reached for it and clicked On. She had no excuse. She was weak. "Paxton?"

"Hi." His voice was masculine and hoarse. Her heart

raced. "I know we agreed to go our separate ways but…
I want to see you."

She wiped sweat from her forehead and said the first
thing that came into her mind. "You said you're not the
staying kind."

"Okay. I'm an idiot."

She laughed. "You are not. You just didn't want to
hurt me. I understood that."

"All I know is I'm not the same man anymore because of you."

Remi gripped the phone. Her heart stilled at his
words. There was no future for them but… Words failed
her and she was glad when he started talking again.

"My dad always said a Rebel loves forever. He said
we would know when we found that special person.
You're my special person. I've been afraid to say it, you
know, because I'm an idiot."

She swung her leg over the bicycle and sat on the
bed. "We barely know each other, and have you forgotten about Annie? Can you see yourself involved with a
woman and a baby?"

"I've been thinking about that. I've never been that
fond of children. But my brothers having kids…it's
changed my outlook. I'd like to meet Annie and I'd
like for us to start seeing each other."

"I don't know what to say." It was everything she
could imagine, having Paxton in her life to help her
with Annie. Could she be that selfish? Or could she
just believe in happy endings?

"I'm coming home in two weeks. I'll come to Houston to see you and we can talk, go out on a date, visit
Annie and see where this journey takes us."

Just say no. End it now.

But her heart wasn't listening. "You want to date a girl who uses a cane?"

"You betcha."

She laughed and there was no way she could refuse. "Okay. We'll take it a step at a time."

"Great. How was your day?"

Remi told him all about her day and he told her about the rodeo. They talked on and on and it was comfortable and easy. She wished she could reach through the phone and touch him. She wondered if he felt the same way.

She clicked off feeling happy. And sad. She still had therapy and the custody hearing ahead of her. Having a normal family was her dream, but there was a world of difference between dreams and reality. And she couldn't help but wonder if Paxton was a reality or a dream.

Chapter Ten

Paxton felt much better after he had talked to Remi. He wanted to explore what they were feeling and he was happy that she did, too. Now he had to put his heart into the rodeo. There were a lot of young guys on the circuit. Brady Haaz was one of them. Paxton liked him. He wasn't arrogant or a show-off. He reminded Paxton of his brother Jude. Brady was quiet, rode his bull and spoke little. He won the second night and Paxton came in second. The young guys were going to dog him this season.

During the night he'd made a decision and Cole and Dakota weren't going to like it. They went out partying again so Paxton had to wait until the morning to talk to them.

They came in at 4:00 a.m. and Paxton woke them up at seven. "It's time to hit the road, boys."

Cole sat up, rubbing his eyes. "We don't have to be in Marshall until—"

"I changed my plans. I'm going home today, then I'll travel to Marshall on Thursday. You can go with me or figure something else out."

Cole swung his feet off the sofa bed, and Dakota finally sat up. "You're our ride, Pax, and our place to sleep. We usually have fun, but you're really putting a damper on the party."

"Sorry, guys."

"That's okay." Dakota crawled out of the bed. "My dad needs help on the ranch, anyway, and that'll give me a couple of days to help him."

They arrived at Rebel Ranch before noon. The trip could have been faster, but Cole and Dakota were hungry and they had to stop for food. After loading their gear in Cole's truck, they talked about the trip to Marshall and Rodeo Austin. They would meet Paxton at Rebel Ranch early Thursday morning.

The ranch was quiet. There weren't many vehicles around, except Elias's and Grandpa's trucks were parked at their house. He supposed everyone was at the hospital visiting the new baby. He planned to be there just as soon as he showered and changed.

He was getting ready to leave again when his mother walked in.

"You're home. Are you hurt?" She looked him up and down. "You don't look hurt."

"I'm not hurt," he told her, easing the worry in her eyes. "I just made a change in my plans. Instead of spending time fooling around with the guys, I plan to see Remi instead."

An eyebrow lifted. "I don't think you gave those feelings enough time to disappear."

"I don't need time."

"I see."

"I'm sorry, Mom."

She waved a hand at him. "I'm not going down that road again, Paxton. It almost broke my heart with Phoenix. You do what makes you happy."

He thought he'd never hear those words from his mother. She detested the McCrays. But there was that thing about time healing all wounds. Even though his mom's grief would never end, she was willing to let her boys live their own lives.

"Thank you."

"I just got back from the hospital. Everyone is doing great."

"I'm on my way there now to see the baby before I go to Houston."

"I'm sure Jenny and Quincy would love that. Take care of yourself."

She went out the door, and before Paxton could follow her, Elias walked in.

"What are you doing home? Did a bull knock you on your head?"

"No, I just had a change of plans."

"Now we're talking." Elias plopped into a chair. "I met this girl and her name is Lilac and her twin sister is Lily. I'm going to meet her tonight, but I need a date for Lily."

"Sorry, Elias. I have other plans."

Elias sat up straight. "Let me tell you what she looks like."

"I'm not interested."

Elias kept talking, as if Paxton hadn't spoken. "She's hot, hot, hot. Smokin' hot."

"Still not interested."

Elias got to his feet. "What did you come home for, then?"

Phoenix saw no reason to lie to his brother. "I have a date with Miss Bertie's granddaughter."

"You mean…"

"Yeah." He really didn't have a date. Remi had no idea he was coming and he knew he should call, but he wanted to surprise her. That might be a mistake he would later regret. He was willing to take his chances, though.

Elias placed his hands on his hips. "Man, wait until Mom hears this. Can't you boys find someone else to date besides a McCray?"

"See you later." Paxton finally made it out the door and was on his way to the hospital. The baby was so small Paxton was afraid of holding her, but Quincy insisted. As he held his niece, he thought about Remi and Annie. Remi had said that Annie was three weeks early and had weighed a little over four pounds. After the surgery, Annie had lost weight and she probably wasn't much bigger now. Fear wedged in his heart. Could he be a good father to a little girl he didn't know, a little girl who wasn't his? Could a man change that much in a few weeks?

IT WAS SUNDAY and Remi had spent the day with her parents. They'd called Gran to talk and asked if Ruger had come back. Remi's mom was really hoping he would be there. But he wasn't.

She had been lazy most of the day and now she had to put some miles on her bicycle. In shorts and a tank top, she rode and rode with Sadie lying beside her. The doorbell rang and she jumped. Who could that be? It might be her neighbor, Mike, who had just moved in a few weeks ago.

She couldn't go to the door in shorts. No one had seen her scars except her parents and Gran. Getting off the bicycle, she reached for her cane and made her way to the door. Looking through the peephole, she froze. A handsome cowboy stood there. Paxton!

What was he doing here? Her heart thumped against her chest and her hands were shaking. She didn't know what to do. She couldn't let him see her like this.

"Give me a minute," she shouted through the door, and hurried to the bedroom to pull on jogging pants.

She took a deep breath to calm herself, then went to let him in. "Paxton, what are you doing here? Shouldn't you be at a rodeo?"

He handed her a bunch of white roses. Until that moment she hadn't noticed them. All she could see was him.

"Oh… Oh…thank you."

He leaned against the doorjamb, looking all cowboy and sexy in his jeans and a white shirt. "Are we going to talk out here or are you going to ask me in?"

"Oh, yes, come in." She stepped aside. Her apartment was a small one-bedroom, much different from her gran's place. She opened the cabinet for a vase, but she couldn't reach it.

He was immediately there to hand it to her.

"Thank you." She arranged the flowers with a nervous hand.

He leaned against the counter, his arms folded across his chest. "Why are we acting like strangers?"

She wiped her hands on her pants. "I'm just surprised to see you."

"Is that good or bad?"

"Good." She looked directly at him. His eyes were warm and inviting and she had a hard time catching her breath.

"We always have a few days between rodeos, and

the guys and I usually just waste time hanging around. This time, I wasn't interested in doing that."

"What are you interested in?" she asked boldly.

"This." He reached out and curled his hand around her neck, and pulled her closer, his lips meeting hers in a hot, sizzling kiss that sent zingers all the way to her toes. She wrapped her arms around his neck and he pulled her even closer against the hard planes of his body. The kiss went on until she thought she would drop to the floor from the sheer pleasure of his lips.

"Paxton," she breathed into his neck. "Touching you—" she ran her hand over the muscles in his shoulder "—and kissing you is wonderful, but we still have the same problems we had two days ago."

He held her by the shoulders to look into her eyes. "We're two grown adults and free to do what we want. I want to spend the next three days with you—getting to know you better, meeting Annie and getting in touch with all these feelings I have when I'm around you. I'm not asking for anything else."

"Aren't you?" She lifted an eyebrow. "You know I'm attracted to you and just standing here breathing the same air as you is making me feel intoxicated."

He didn't even pause with his words. "I admit I've never gone out with a girl this long without sleeping with her, but I respect your wishes. When you're ready, you'll tell me. I'm not going to push you."

She rested her forehead on his chest. "Paxton, it's not that I don't want to have sex. It's just that I haven't since the accident and I—"

"It's okay." He kissed her lips. "Like I said, when you're ready." He looked toward the living area. "Do you mind if I sleep on your couch?"

She glanced up at him. "So the plan is to spend time together away from Horseshoe and our families?"

"Yeah. Time together without any interruptions."

"That sounds…" She grinned. "Like fun. I'd love to spend time with you. So, you can sleep on my couch, but let's have dinner first." She moved toward the stove.

"Let's go out," he suggested. "It's not late."

She made a face at him. "I'm all sweaty from exercise and I'd rather stay in."

He winked. "You got it."

"How about spaghetti?"

"I grew up on SpaghettiOs, so anything with sauce on it works for me."

He helped her to prepare the meal and she found a bottle of wine. They sat in comfortable silence eating and she loved being with him again. *Love.* The word lingered in her mind like a favorite melody, making her aware of her feelings.

She loved him.

WHILE PAXTON DID the dishes, Remi quickly took a shower and then sat on the commode to rub lotion onto her body. Every night she used a special cream to rub on the scars.

Paxton was here. Her hands shook at the anticipation. She loved him and the feminine side of her was grabbing at everything he offered. Three days together could be heaven. All she had to do was not be so uptight about her injuries.

She slipped on fresh jogging pants and a T-shirt. Usually she slept in just a T-shirt. She took a deep breath and went down the hall to a closet and got a blanket and a pillow for Paxton.

In the living room he sat on the sofa. He'd removed his boots and his shirt was unbuttoned, revealing a broad chest and a light smattering of chest hair. Her brain completely shut down at the sight.

He glanced at the jogging pants. "Do you usually wear those to bed?"

It took a moment for her to answer. "No."

"Why do you have them on tonight?"

"They cover my scars. I'm very self-conscious about them."

"What?" He frowned. "You think if I see them, I'll run screaming into the night?"

She stiffened her backbone. "I'll never know because I'll never show them to you. Only my family and the people at the hospital have seen them."

His eyes held hers for a long time. "Remi, the scars don't matter to me."

She handed him the blanket and pillow. "If you need anything else, there's more in the hall closet."

"It really doesn't matter to me," he said again, and she walked away to her bedroom with Sadie trailing behind her. She sat on her bed with the door closed, feeling naive and insecure. Try as she might she couldn't get over it; she couldn't. She wasn't the same as she was before the accident and she didn't want anyone to see her this way, especially Paxton, who was beyond physically perfect.

The fear deep inside her wouldn't let go. Since all the internal surgeries, sex would be different now. Or at least everything she'd read had said so and she wanted everything to be wonderful with Paxton. What was she going to do? Was she going to let fear control her? Or take back her life?

She glanced at the baby bed in the room and all of Annie's things. She wanted Paxton to be a part of their lives. So many doubts and fears fought for control inside her, but above everything she wanted to be with him. Sadie jumped onto the bed, and Remi pointed to Sadie's bed.

"No, not tonight. Get in your bed." With a whine, Sadie did as Remi requested.

Sucking air into her tight lungs, she opened the door and walked into the living room. The room was in total darkness, but she could see Paxton lying on the sofa covered with a blanket.

He sat up when he noticed her.

"Something wrong?"

"I'm ready," she said with every ounce of bravado she had in her.

"What?"

She didn't think she would have to explain it, but obviously he was confused. "You said when I was ready, I would tell you. I'm ready."

"Oh." He quickly pushed back the blanket and got to his feet in nothing but jockey briefs. "Are you sure? You said—"

"Paxton." She sighed.

"Okay. I just want you to be sure."

"I'm sure."

Still he hesitated. "So this means you're going to let me see your scars?"

"Not if you don't come over here and kiss every doubt away."

It took him less time than an eight-second bull ride. He swung her up into his arms and carried her into the bedroom and carefully sat her on the bed. Her breath stalled at his gentleness and caring.

Leaning over, he kissed her lips as warmly as a summer breeze. Without any doubts, she stood up and removed her jogging pants. Her legs felt weak and she sat down again. The fire in his eyes was turning up the heat in her.

He knelt at her feet and she wanted to cry at the action. While he gazed at her left leg, she held her breath, resisting the urge to turn away. That moment was over. With one long finger, he trailed the scars from her hip down to below her knee. His hand felt like a velvet glove.

Leaning back on his heels, he said, "What's the big deal? It's a scar—several scars and a burned area. People have seen scars before." He pointed to the calf of his right leg. "A bull gored me there and left a scar. I don't even think about it being there anymore, nor do I care."

"It's different for a woman and I wanted to be perfect for you."

"I'm not perfect, Remi. I don't require the girls I date to be perfect, either."

She titled her head with a mischievous grin. "You're making me crazy, do you know that?"

The corners of his mouth turned up a notch. "Then let's stop talking." In one movement he scooped her up and slid into the bed with her. His hard, firm body was touching all the right places and rational thought was floating away quickly.

"Paxton," she murmured as his lips trailed from her cheek to her neck.

He raised his head to look into her eyes. "Don't say

a word. I want us to go with this moment because it's what we both want."

He took her lips in a passionate kiss and all thoughts disappeared like tiny puffs of smoke. All that mattered was his hand, his lips and his body taking hers on a journey she'd long forgotten. Paxton awoke every nerve she had in her body and she moaned as he touched her intimately. Her hands reached for him and her fingertips greedily caressed his hard muscles. He had to be the most perfect man alive.

She forgot about her leg. She forgot about everything but the touch of him. When he entered her, she gasped from the sheer pleasure of it and everything she'd been missing. It was clear that Paxton knew what he was doing and took care to be gentle while still arousing her to fever pitch. The journey ended in the deepest pleasure of all as her body trembled.

Paxton's body shook and she held on as the remnants of pleasure began to fade away. He raised his head to look at her. His hair fell across his forehead and his eyes were as dark as midnight. "I love you, Remi. Really. Really. Really."

"I *really* love you, too." She didn't even hesitate in responding. For now the fairy tale was real.

He laughed softly, tucking her into the side of his sweat-bathed body. As he kissed her forehead, the world tilted the right way for the first time in months.

Chapter Eleven

Paxton got up and turned off the light. They'd been so enthralled with each other they hadn't even noticed it was still on. He took note of the crib and baby things. She was ready to become a mother and he hoped he was ready to be a part of it. There was still a worry in his mind about fatherhood.

He crawled back into bed and reached for the sheet and comforter to pull over them. Remi was sound asleep. He carefully gathered her into his arms and felt complete in a way he never had before. And it was very clear to him why. He'd just made love to a woman he loved and it was an awakening to a whole new world of emotions. All the girls before her were just mindless sex. Maybe he was the scoundrel he'd been called.

He wished he could make Remi believe how beautiful she was, scars and all. Her skin was the softest thing he'd ever touched, smooth and silky. He would never get tired of touching her. When he'd cupped her breasts, his world had rocked a little. They were perfect.

For a man who was known for choosing beautiful women, he found it refreshing that he had chosen the most beautiful one of all. Not only was she beautiful on the outside, but she had an inner beauty, too. And he vowed to spend the rest of his life making her happy.

Tucking her hair behind her ear, he couldn't even imagine the pain and suffering she'd been through. Whatever she had to go through in the future he would be there to help her. There was something to be said about change. It made a man think and tonight as he held her close he felt good about himself. He felt good about the future.

THE BUZZ OF a cell phone woke them. Paxton groaned, and Remi sat up. "Where's my phone?"

Paxton reached to the nightstand and handed it to her. "Oh, no. What time is it? I missed my therapy session." She hurriedly clicked on. "Hi, Chad. I'm sorry—" she glanced at Paxton "—I had a friend over and went to bed late and overslept."

Paxton cupped a breast and ran a finger over her nipple just to watch her face.

She caught his hand. "Stop it," she mouthed.

"Okay. Two o'clock will be fine. I'll see you then." She looked at Paxton. "You're in big trouble, mister."

Paxton's attention was on Remi's closet. The doors were open and the racks on the doors were stacked with shoes. Shoes were everywhere on the floor. Every height of high heels imaginable were there and flats and other shoes, too.

"Do you house shoes for women?" he asked with a mischievous grin.

She slapped his arm. "Of course not. Those are my shoes, but… I'll never be able to wear them again. I have to give them away soon. I love to wear my boots in the winter with long skirts. The doctor said a half inch is probably all I should wear. So goodbye shoes. And I need more room for Annie's stuff, too."

At the sadness in her voice, he pulled her down on top of him, the cell phone falling to the bed. Every girl should have boots and he was going to make sure Remi had a good pair. He had a rodeo friend who owned a boot-making company and Paxton was certain the man could make something perfect for Remi. He would keep it as a surprise for her birthday, which was coming up soon. He'd heard Miss Bertie talking about it.

"Paxton, we have to go. It's almost eleven in the morning," she breathed in between breathless kisses.

"Do you really want to stop?" he asked, staring into the glow of her green eyes.

Thirty minutes later they were rushing for the shower. Remi had to feed Sadie. Paxton had to shave. He got a glimpse of what it would be like living with a woman. The bathroom smelled like perfume and he wasn't complaining. It was just different. It was twelve thirty when they stepped out of the apartment. After a late breakfast, they drove to Chad's clinic, which was near the Houston Medical Center.

At the center, Paxton met Chad, Remi's therapist. Paxton thought he was just a little too young and had too many muscles. But he seemed nice.

After the introduction, Paxton said, "Remi is doing better and better."

Chad glanced at Remi. "Yes, she is, but she still has a ways to go." He took Remi's elbow and made to walk off to a hall to the right.

"Do you mind if I tag along?"

Chad looked perplexed until Remi spoke up. "Please

let him sit in," she said. "He pushes me just like you do." She held up the cane. "See, he has me using this."

"I guess it would be okay. Just don't interfere."

Paxton sat in a chair with Sadie beside him while Remi worked out with weights and on an elliptical machine with Chad giving her orders. Then they went to a workout table where she did stretches and more weights. They did exercises for balance and just about a little bit of everything. He couldn't fault Chad for his technique. Then Chad had Remi kneel on the padded table. Her face scrunched into a painful mask. Paxton was instantly on his feet, but he held his tongue.

"Breathe in and out," Chad was saying. "The pain will get better. Slowly, try to lean back on your heels."

Sweat broke out on Remi's forehead.

Paxton bit his tongue. He'd promised not to interfere, but clearly Remi was in pain.

"It hurts," Remi said in a low voice.

Paxton couldn't take it anymore. He walked over and sat on the mat with Remi. A cold stare from Chad was his reward.

"You can do it," Paxton said to Remi. "I'm right here." The scars on her left leg were now red and she was breathing heavily. He stroked her tight calf and she leaned back with a scream that came out muffled.

"Great!" Chad clapped.

Remi fell forward on the mat and just lay there. Paxton stroked her wet hair. "You did it. The pain will get better just as Chad said."

She opened one eye to look at him. "If I didn't love you so much, I'd really be mad."

The rest of the afternoon went smoothly. They went back to the apartment so Remi could shower and change. A nurse that Remi knew agreed to let them see Annie.

Hand in hand they walked down the hall at Texas Children's Hospital. It was at the Houston Medical Center and devoted to the care and healing of children. Annie's room was right across from the nurse's station.

"A lot of the children have parents or family who stay with them, but Annie has no one, so the nurses take care of her," Remi told him.

They'd passed a playroom and he'd noticed some children playing with brightly colored toys in the room. Some were in wheelchairs. It was heartbreaking and it touched him. This was part of the life he'd been isolated from and it brought home just what a selfish way he'd been living.

A nurse in scrubs came down the hall to meet them. Remi hugged her. "Thank you for letting us see Annie." She turned to Paxton. "This is Paxton Rebel."

Paxton shook her hand. "Nice to meet you."

"You, too," the nurse said with a smile. They followed her into a room. A little girl about three months old lay inside of a large baby bed. A big pink bow adorned her blond hair, which had a slight curl. Lying on her back, she kicked out with her arms and legs.

Remi immediately went to the bed. "Hi, precious."

The little girl kicked that much faster, looking at Remi. A smile split her face and Remi reached down and picked her up. Paxton stood beside Remi in case she needed help. "How are you?" She kissed Annie's cheek.

Annie laid her head on Remi's shoulder and the affectionate response caused tears to well up in Remi's eyes. He put his arm around her waist until Annie raised her head to look at him.

"This is Paxton," Remi said to Annie.

Annie reached out for him and he caught her hand. She wrapped her fingers around his, and he fell in love all over again. The one thing he noticed through all the emotions that swelled inside him was Annie's eyes were green, almost like Remi's.

"She's getting so big," Remi said.

"What?" Annie was tiny to him, but this was his first time meeting her.

"I told you she was so small at birth and then she lost some weight after the surgery. I'm happy to see her gaining weight now."

"Does she have special medical needs?" he asked, wanting to know everything about the little girl.

"She has to have regular heart checkups, but she's fine now, the doctors say. She can even play sports if she wants."

"She seems happy."

"She always perks up when Remi comes," Sandy said. "I told Ms. Connors from CPS about that. I'm in your corner on this. All the nurses are."

"Thank you, Sandy."

Remi sat with Annie in a rocker and they stayed until Annie fell asleep. Remi would make a good mother and he could see how much she loved that little girl. CPS had to see it, too. Paxton put the sleeping baby back into the crib because Remi was afraid to stand up with the baby in her arms. He looked into her sea-green eyes and all of his worries and doubts about loving Annie disappeared. He could do this. He could be a father to this little girl.

Remi was quiet on the way home. He reached out and took her hand. "Stop worrying. Everyone at the hospital knows who Annie belongs with and soon CPS will, too." He squeezed her hand. "Do you have a lawyer?"

"Yes. She said my chances are good because I was Holly's best friend and Annie and I have bonded. But my health will be a concern."

He pulled into the parking lot of an office building so he could talk to her. "I had my doubts about Annie. Well, not about her, but about me being a father to her."

Remi's eyes opened wide.

"I'm in this forever. I want us to get married and be a family."

"What?"

"That's what I'm thinking. What are you thinking?"

She reached across the console and wrapped her arms around his neck. "I think you're the most amazing man ever."

Thirty minutes later they sat in Remi's lawyer's office, but they didn't get the news they were hoping for.

"I think it's a good thing you've found someone, Remi," Constance Baxter said. A woman in her midfifties with graying blond hair, Ms. Baxter was all business. "But it's not going to help the custody hearing at this late date. It's like pulling a rabbit out of a hat sort of thing and the judge is not going to go for it. She'll think the marriage is phony. I will let the court know you're in a committed relationship, though. It will be good to show you're moving on with your life and your therapy. That's the most important thing, Remi. You have to be able to pick Annie up from the floor and carry her around confidently. So far, you haven't been able to do that. I send over weekly health reports and have affidavits from all your teacher friends at the school saying Holly would have wanted you to have Annie. None of that matters unless you can physically take care of the baby on your own."

"Isn't there anything we can do?" Paxton asked.

"Just stay positive. This all takes time, so hang in there." She smiled at Paxton. "And congratulations. You're good for Remi. She's positively glowing."

On the way home Remi was quiet again and it tore at his heart. "I'm starving," he said as a way to get her attention off Annie.

She smiled at him and everything was right in his world. "How about pizza?"

He winked at her, and she leaned over and kissed his cheek. Paxton drove on, hating that Wednesday would come sooner than he wanted. How was he going to leave her and go back to the rodeo circuit?

THE NEXT FEW days were the happiest of Remi's life. She spent every moment with Paxton, whom she'd come to love more than life itself. They talked about marriage and, since it wouldn't help with the adoption, decided to wait until rodeo season was over. And they also decided not to tell anyone, especially Remi's parents. Her mother would go bonkers with excitement and she wanted time with Paxton to be just the two of them. And Annie.

Sandy set up two more visits with Annie, and Paxton was enthralled with the baby. Remi had no doubts they could make the relationship work. Her deepest fears disappeared and she lived in her fairy tale wholeheartedly.

They spent a lot of time in the apartment, but they did go out a couple of times. Paxton bought a kite and they flew it in a park, but it got caught in a tree and she laughed as he climbed up to get it. They laughed a lot, something she hadn't done in months, but Wednesday soon arrived and they would have to let go for now. They went out to lunch and then decided to spend the rest of the day in the apartment.

After a rigorous afternoon of lovemaking, they sat on the sofa, holding each other. The doorbell sounded, jarring both of them. Paxton hurried to the door to look through the peephole.

"It's a man and a woman. I think it might be your parents."

"Oh, no." Remi went as fast as she could to the bedroom for jogging pants and a tank top while Paxton slipped into his jeans.

"Coming!" she called loudly.

She looked back at Paxton, who was buttoning his shirt. "Ready?"

He nodded and she opened the door. Her parents stood there, looking surprised. They were dressed as usual. Her dad had on his suit pants and dress shirt. Her mom wore a blue print dress with heels. Each had something in their hands.

"Hi, sweetheart," her mother said. "I made chicken spaghetti with garlic bread." She held up the bread wrapped in tinfoil and her dad held up a covered dish.

"Aren't you going to ask us in?" her dad asked as Remi continued to block the doorway.

"Oh. I'm sorry." She stood aside for her parents to enter the apartment. She wasn't embarrassed; she was still in shock.

"Oh." Her mother paused as she noticed Paxton. "We didn't know you had company. I called and you didn't answer your phone and that had me worried."

"It's okay, Mom." She held a hand toward Paxton. "This is Paxton Rebel. He stopped by for a visit."

Her mother gave Paxton the once-over. "I'd forgotten how handsome Kate's sons were."

"Ava, really," her dad teased, and took the food into the kitchen. In a second he was back and held out his hand to Paxton. "I'm Nathan, Remi's father, and it's nice to meet you."

Paxton shook his hand. "It's nice to meet you, too, sir."

Her dad took her mother's arm. "And now we'll leave you young people to enjoy your evening."

Ava pulled her arm away. "Just a minute, Nathan. I want to meet this young man our daughter is dating." Her eyes narrowed on Paxton. "Don't you feel strange dating my daughter, a McCray?"

"No, ma'am, I don't. Remi and I discussed the past and decided to let it go."

"How does your mother feel about this?"

Remi had had enough. "Mom, you're sticking your nose in again, and I would appreciate it if you would stop the grilling."

"I'm sorry, sweetheart," her mother said, and held out her hand to Paxton. "I tend to go overboard when it concerns my daughter."

Paxton took her hand and said, "I would never hurt Remi."

"I will hold you to that." Before her mother could say anything else, her father took her arm once again and led her from the apartment.

Remi and Paxton fell onto the sofa laughing. After a moment, they sobered up and Remi said, "Did you feel as if you were in a police station?"

"Almost, but I know where she's coming from. She cares about you."

"I know." She rested against him and felt the beat of his heart. A tiny movement that made her feel…loved. With Paxton, she had no fears, life was too good.

"I have an idea." He tucked hair behind her ear. "Why don't we eat that spaghetti and go to bed."

Forty-five minutes later they were tucked in for the night. At four in the morning Paxton would leave for Rebel Ranch to pick up his trailer and then he would meet up with his friends for the trip to Marshall, Texas. She awoke when he crawled out of bed.

She pushed hair from her face. "Is it time?"

"Yes." He didn't turn on the light as he slipped into his clothes. "My bag is packed and I'm leaving for now. You'll have to lock the door and put on the chain."

"Kiss me goodbye first."

"I'll never kiss you goodbye" was his surprising answer.

"Paxton."

"No touching. No kissing. Or I will never get out of here."

She knew he had commitments and she wouldn't tempt him. But it was hard not to reach for him.

"I'll text later. It will be hard to talk on the phone with the guys around but I'll find a way."

"Drive carefully," she called as he went through the door. "And good luck." She dragged herself out of bed and went to put on the chain. A loneliness settled over her as she trailed back to her room. Snuggling beneath the covers, she reached for his pillow. His aftershave clung to it lightly, and she breathed in the scent. He was still here. She could feel him.

Paxton made her feel alive again, all woman and even beautiful at times. He loved Annie as she did.

All her dreams had come true. At the back of her mind was a niggling reminder that dreams don't come true. She was mature enough to know that, but for now she was living the fairy tale and she couldn't make herself do anything else.

She loved him.

PAXTON MADE IT to the ranch a little after six. The light was on in the bunkhouse, so Rico was up. Paxton had already done his laundry at Remi's. All he had to do now was get the trailer ready and load his duffel bag with his bull ropes. He was ready to hit the road as soon as his friends arrived.

The sound of the truck caught Paxton's attention. "See you later, Rico," he called, going out the door as Rico fixed breakfast. Paxton would eat with Cole and Dakota.

"Good luck!" Rico shouted after him.

Within minutes they were on the road again. As Paxton drove over the cattle guard, the sun rose in the east, kind of slow and lazy. It was going to be another cool March day.

It was a four-hour drive and Paxton let Cole drive for a while. Paxton was back at the wheel as they drove into Marshall and the rodeo arena.

"Barron's gonna ride at this rodeo, too," Cole announced.

"So is Brady and Trey Goodready," Dakota spoke up from the backseat. "There's another new guy named Clint Hightower. I think he's about nineteen. Where are all these young guys coming from? And what kind of name is Goodready?"

"They say he's good and ready all the time," Cole

said. "And he's probably going to show us just how good and ready he is."

There were a lot of new guys on the circuit and they were keeping pace with the older ones. They were big competition for Paxton and he had to stay focused. That was hard when all his thoughts were on Remi. He had texted her several times to keep up with what she was doing and just to talk to her. He never knew love would be like this—that it would hurt. It hurt to be away from her.

Chapter Twelve

Remi stayed busy working with Chad. Every day they went through the same routine and every day Chad pushed her just a little more. She was now able to kneel without a lot of pain. The stretches helped to loosen up her tight muscles. To be healthy again she had to keep working.

One afternoon she visited her school and the children she'd taught and enjoyed every minute of it. Next year she would have a whole new class of shining, fresh faces. Afterward she went to dinner with one of her teacher friends. They talked about Holly and Annie and Remi told her about Paxton. It was good to talk about him. She missed him. Her favorite part of the day was getting home and waiting for Paxton to call. They spent endless hours on the phone.

One night she waited and waited for his call, but it never came. Then she got a text: Open the door. It was Paxton, and she flew into his arms. Just being with him made her giddy. At 6:00 a.m. he had to leave again and she held on just a little tighter this time. The long periods of not seeing him were getting hard.

DURING THE WEEK Remi got a call from her lawyer. CPS had found a distant cousin of Holly's who was interested in Annie. Kelly and Jim Wallace lived in Houston and Remi found it odd that Holly had never mentioned her cousin. The couple had filed for permanent custody. Remi was a nervous wreck and called Paxton.

"How is this woman related?"

"Holly's dad had been married before and had a daughter who was twelve years older than Holly's mother. When the half sister married, she moved away. Holly mentioned once she had an aunt in Oregon whom she'd never met. CPS did a lot of checking for relatives of Holly and Derek's. The half sister said she was too old to raise a baby, as did her daughter. It's the daughter of the daughter who's interested in Annie. She's had three miscarriages and now the couple has decided to adopt."

"You have a much stronger connection to Annie and your health is so much better. Just say positive."

"I'll try. But now that Annie no longer needs medical attention the judge has ruled that she be moved into foster care temporarily until the final ruling is made. The decision will be between me and the Wallaces. The good thing is Ms. Baxter asked for visitation rights and the judge granted it. I'll still get to see Annie, as does Kelly and her husband."

"I'm glad. Just remember I love you and we'll get through this."

That was all she needed to hear to face the future.

LATER, REMI GOT a call from her grandmother. Ruger wanted to see his mother. Remi couldn't be happier and she needed a break from everything that was happening with Annie. She quickly made arrangements with her mother to go to Horseshoe. She left a message for Paxton to let him know where she would be. Almost instantly she got a text: I'll meet you there. Going home for a couple of days. That made the trip just perfect.

Gran had made a big lunch and they sat around waiting. It was almost twelve when Ruger showed up. He was clean-shaven and even had a new haircut. His clothes were clean, too. It was a tense moment as he looked at everyone, cautious of what to say, Remi was sure. She walked up and hugged him and said, "Welcome home."

Her mother, unable to stay quiet any longer, hugged her son and surprisingly Ruger hugged her back. She introduced Nathan and they sat on the sofa talking like families should.

It was plain to see her brother had a lot on his mind. "Paxton Rebel's story of Dad's murder was different than what Uncle Ira had told me. I didn't know who to believe so I went to the courthouse and looked up the records. What I read was everything that the Rebel boy had said." He turned to look at his mother. "Why would Dad try to kill two little boys?"

Ava rubbed her son's back. Remi knew it was a gesture to remind him of all the beatings he'd had at the hands of his father.

"A lot of people in Horseshoe asked the same question. But they knew the answer, as I did, and Kate and John Rebel did, too."

Remi sat up a little straighter in her chair. Her mother had never spoken about the reason Ezra McCray had shot Jude and Phoenix and she was very curious.

"Why?" Ruger asked.

"Your father was obsessed with Kate. She moved to Horseshoe her senior year and she was new and all the boys were eager to meet her. Ezra was one of them. He asked her out time and time again and she always refused. He became infatuated with her and followed her everywhere, even changing his school schedule to fit hers. He basically harassed her until her mother contacted the sheriff. He couldn't do much but I think Ezra let up on following her after the sheriff had talked to him. But it escalated again when Kate started dating John. They got into a fight and John bloodied Ezra's nose. Ezra threatened to kill him if he ever went near Kate again. Of course, John didn't listen. They got married right out of high school and Ezra became maniacal, wanting to get even."

Her mother glanced down at her hands, which were clasped tightly in her lap. No one moved or said a word as they waited for her to start talking again. "Sadly, his way to get even was to marry someone else. Even sadder was he chose a stupid girl who was so gullible that she believed every word he said. We would build a big house and travel and I would have everything I ever wanted. I was eager to get away from home so I married him."

Gran made a disgusting sound in her throat, but Remi's attention was on her mother.

Ava wiped away a tear, and Remi got up and went to sit beside her. "It was hell from the very first day. I wanted to leave, but Ezra threatened to kill me if I ever left him. He wasn't over Kate. He kept pictures of her in a drawer. And when Kate and John's sons were born, he became even crazier. He met John in town one day. I was sitting in the truck and heard every word. He said if any of those little bastards ever crossed over onto McCray property he would kill them. He meant every word. He was just waiting for them to cross the line. When I heard what had happened and that Ezra was dead, I didn't feel any sadness or grief. I felt relief. And..." Her mother buried her face in her hands and began to cry.

Remi put her arms around her mother. "Please don't. No one blames you."

Her dad came over and knelt at Ava's feet. "Honey, it's over. Like Remi said, no one blames you."

"But I lost my son. No one knows how that feels."

"I'm sorry, Mom." Ruger hugged his mother. "I'm sorry."

Gran got to her feet. "Enough with all these tears. Let's bury the past for good. We're back together and we're going to stay that way." She marched toward the kitchen. "I have chicken and dressing and all the trimmings so let's dive in. I want to see some smiles."

They had a nice meal, and although they would never be a normal family, at least they were a family. They could build on that. As Remi ate, she thought about her mother's story and she wondered if Paxton knew Ezra McCray had been in love with his mother. She had to wipe it from her mind, but it kept springing up at the oddest of times, especially when Paxton arrived later.

After supper, she and Paxton sat on the swing. Gran was asleep in her chair and her parents and Ruger had left a long time ago.

"You're quiet tonight," Paxton said with his arm around her. "Are you worried about the hearing?"

She snuggled into him. "A little. It's just been a long day."

"But you said everything went really well."

"It did." She smiled at him. Nothing was going to ruin her time with Paxton. "After Gran goes to bed, we can sneak into my bedroom like teenagers."

He kissed her deeply, and she moaned, enjoying being back with him. How she wished life could stay this way.

"Did you give Annie a kiss from me?"

"Of course I did." She snuggled against him. "When I kiss her now, she puts her face against mine as if she's trying to kiss me back. She's doing so many new things."

"Did you meet the cousin?"

"Yes, briefly at the temporary hearing. She seemed nice, but nervous. My lawyer said I still have a better chance since she and Holly weren't close."

"And the permanent custody hearing will take a couple of months?"

She looked up at him. "Yes, and I'm looking at it as a good thing. It gives me more time to get healthy. As I told you on the phone, I can stand up from the floor by myself, but I can't with anything in my arms. Chad and I are still working on that and he feels confident that I will be able to do it eventually. And I've gained five more pounds."

"Whoa, that's—"

Lights from a truck crossing the cattle guard flashed on them. "Who could that be?" Remi asked. As the truck drove into the front yard, Remi could see it was Ruger. "Wonder why he's come back?"

Paxton shrugged and they got to their feet as Ruger came up the steps. He had something in his hand and held it out to Remi. "Mom mentioned the diamond necklace Gran and Pa had given her for graduation today. She said she couldn't find it when she left. I found it." He held it up. "I thought she might want it back."

"Oh, Ruger. That's so sweet. She said she loved that

necklace. It was the first diamond she ever had. I'll make sure she gets it, or why don't you wait until she comes to Horseshoe again and you can give it to her yourself?"

Ruger shook his head. "I don't know. It will probably make her cry and I don't like it when she cries. I'd rather you gave it to her."

"Okay." Remi took the necklace. Ruger was still resisting, but he was coming more and more to Gran's so that had to mean something. And the fact that he had looked for the necklace meant a whole lot more.

Ruger eyed Paxton. "Why didn't you tell me my father was in love with your mother?"

No! No! No! Remi didn't know what to do, but she knew this was bad for Paxton to hear it this way. But maybe he already knew…

"Everybody in town knows the story, Ruger. You need to start listening to someone other than your uncle Ira. Talk to some of the older people who were around at that time."

"I don't like to talk to people."

"Then you'll never know the truth."

"I'll see y'all later." Ruger went down the steps without another word.

Remi stroked Paxton's chest. "So you knew about my father and your mother?"

"Everyone does, Remi. He made my parents' lives miserable."

"But yet, you love his daughter."

He smiled into her eyes and everything was much brighter. "Yes, ma'am."

She stroked his face. "I'm so tired of all the bitterness

and hatred between the Rebels and McCrays. I just want it to end. And I don't want it to affect our relationship."

"Me, neither," Paxton said.

She kissed his cold lips. "We won't let it." His hand slid beneath her T-shirt to cup her breast, and desire uncurled in her stomach. "Let's sneak into the house."

He laughed that deep sound she loved and everything melted away but him and their feelings. The way it should be.

IN LATE APRIL, Remi was excited out of her mind when Paxton told her he was coming back to Texas to rodeo and he would have time to visit her and Annie. It had been so long since she'd seen him, so she decided to make the trip to Longview, Texas, to watch Paxton ride.

It was a little disconcerting to sit in the stands and watch all the girls shouting, "Paxton!" Some of them even had T-shirts with his name on them. They were screaming and yelling, standing on their feet, especially when he rode. Remi stood, too, with her heart in her throat. The bull seemed so big and dangerous yet Paxton was steadfast. She clapped like all the others when he made the ride.

She hurried to meet him near the loading chutes. Her balance was so much better and she was walking without the cane. Her strength was better, too, as was her state of mind. The scent of manure, animals and sweat assaulted her senses, but she kept walking.

When Paxton saw her, he immediately came toward her and gathered her into his arms. She rested against him as if she needed him to breathe. He took her hand and led her through the starry night to his trailer.

She stepped inside and looked around. "So this is it? This is where you live on the road?"

He bowed from the waist in a mock gesture. "Yes, ma'am." He pointed toward a bed. "And that's where we'll sleep."

"What about your friends?"

"I told them to find someplace else to sleep tonight. Anyway, they'll be out partying. And we'll be alone." As he talked, he walked slowly toward her until he was standing next to her, touching her body. He swung her into his arms and carried her to the bed and she got lost in the magic of being with him again.

They spent the morning together and she met his friends, Cole and Dakota. Cole was lean with brown hair and brown eyes while Dakota was muscled with dark hair and blue eyes. They kidded and teased her about Paxton and told stories that raised her eyebrows. She liked Paxton's friends. She left after lunch and it was another sad parting.

Back in Houston, it was the same old routine of therapy and visiting Annie. One evening in May she got a call from Ms. Baxter. It had to be news about the hearing. It was.

"I just wanted to let you know Hazel Connors from CPS called and she said the judge is making the decision on Annie in the next couple of days." She gave Remi the date, time and where to go. "Please don't be late. The judge's docket is full and if we miss our time, it will be rescheduled."

"I won't. Thank you."

"Remi, I want you to be prepared either way." They talked for a minute more and Remi clicked off. She sank to the sofa. *Either way.* No, there was only one way. She'd waited months for this and had even gotten another medical report in, hoping that would help the judge to make the right decision. She just had to wait.

First, she had to call Paxton.

Chapter Thirteen

It was the last night of a rodeo in Helotes, Texas. Weary to the bone, Paxton grabbed his duffel bag and headed for the trailer. Cole and Dakota were talking to some girls. They were supposed to leave early in the morning for Oklahoma and he hoped they weren't going to pull an all-nighter. He didn't plan on driving the whole distance.

He put them out of his mind as he hurried to call Remi. Getting comfortable on the bed, his cell buzzed.

It was Remi.

"Hey, beautiful. What's up?"

"I know your schedule is packed and I don't want you to worry, but Ms. Baxter called and said the judge is going to make the decision about Annie. I can handle it. I'll call and let you know if we have a daughter."

"That's sooner than we expected."

"Yes. I'm hoping that's a good sign."

"I should be there."

"I understand you have commitments and I'm fine. As soon as the hearing is over, I'll call you."

"Remi…"

"I'm fine."

Paxton wasn't so sure. She sounded nervous, but

she was stronger now. Maybe she could handle it if the judge awarded custody to the Wallaces. At that thought he wondered if *he* could. Long after they ended the call, he lay in bed and wished he could be in two places at one time. Because he knew one thing—Remi didn't need to be alone when she heard the decision whether it was good or bad. By morning he had it figured out.

He woke Cole and Dakota at 5:00 a.m. They'd returned to the trailer right after he had so they'd had enough sleep.

Cole crawled out of bed, blinking his eyes. "It's still dark outside. What's the deal?"

"I have to go to Houston."

"What!" Cole was wide-awake now.

Dakota sat up. "Oh, man, that girl has you tied up in knots."

"It's about the baby. The judge is going to award custody and I have to be there if things go wrong." He'd told his friends about Annie and his and Remi's hopes of adopting her.

Paxton squatted to show them his phone. "Here's the plan. We're going to leave here and drive to Cole's dad's ranch. We'll hook the travel trailer to Cole's truck and y'all can go on to Oklahoma. I'll travel to Houston to see what's happening and meet you guys in Oklahoma in time for the rodeo."

"Okay." Cole scratched his head. "What are y'all gonna do if you don't get custody?"

"I don't know." He would just be there for Remi because it was going to be hard on both of them.

Going to pick up Cole's truck was a little out of the way, but Paxton made it to Remi's apartment before noon. He was hoping she was home. He pulled out his phone and called her.

"Where are you?"

"I just got out of the shower from therapy. Why?"

"Open the door."

"Paxton."

"Open the door." The door swung open and all she had on was a towel. Her hair was wet and combed back from her face and for a moment he couldn't catch his breath. He'd seen her like this so many times and it still revved up his blood pressure a few notches. Forgetting everything else, he took her in his arms and kissed her until they were both breathless.

"I love this kind of surprise," she whispered into his neck.

Over her shoulder he could see the couch and on it was a pink-and-white baby outfit with shoes, a big bow, a blanket and several other things. "Been shopping, huh?" he asked.

She turned in the circle of his arms to stare at the couch. "Oh. I bought some things for Annie. She's outgrowing everything."

She leaned against him, and he wrapped his arms around her, pulling her damp body close to his. Once again everything else was forgotten and he did what every cowboy would do in this situation. He swung her into his arms and carried her to the bedroom. Nothing was said for some time.

Scooting up against the headboard, he noticed her closet. All the high heels were gone. "What happened to the shoes?"

Remi cuddled against him. "I took them to the nurses at the hospital and they went crazy over them. I'm glad someone is going to use them now. I kept my boots, though."

He nibbled on her lips. "You're about the sweetest thing ever. When I kiss you, I can taste it."

Remi laughed and it was good to hear that sound because he had a feeling it was going to be a long day. "Have you heard anything else from Ms. Baxter?" His stomach tied into one big knot. The judge's decision had to go the way they'd planned. Their whole future depended on it.

She played with the hair on his chest. "No."

That one word sounded so forlorn and his heart took a hit. They needed a diversion. "I'm hungry. Have you got anything to eat?"

She lifted an eyebrow. "You're always ravenous."

"Yes, ma'am."

She climbed out of bed with a smile and reached for a T-shirt. "Mom brought over a casserole. I think she's afraid I might starve 'cause she's always bringing food."

Reaching for his jeans, he said, "I'll meet you in the kitchen."

With everything on the table, they sat down to eat. Little was said during the meal. He asked about therapy and Remi told him how well she was doing. There was a tension and awkwardness in her voice. It was clear she was very nervous about the decision and he had to bring it up.

He leaned back in his chair. "Honey, we have to be prepared."

She smiled at him. "That's the first time you've called me honey."

"Well, you are my honey."

"Yes, I am." She leaned across the table to kiss him

and he wanted to go on kissing her, but he was getting sidetracked.

"Whatever happens, you and I are still a couple. You and I are still in love. You and I still have a future." He wanted her to understand that.

She sat back with a thoughtful expression on her pretty face. "I can handle this, Paxton. But I know Annie belongs with us. They have to do the right thing."

"Honey…" He wanted her to be prepared, but he just couldn't burst her bubble. Besides, he wanted Annie, too, and he was praying with everything in him that Remi's positive attitude would help.

They spent the night in each other's arms and by morning they were ready to face whatever happened. Weeks of wondering and worrying had come down to this, and soon they would know if Annie would be their little girl.

As THEY STEPPED into the family court room Remi was surprised at all the people standing around talking as if this was a social event. They sat by Ms. Baxter and she told them after they were called it would only take a few minutes.

Judge Frances Tomlin heard case after case, seemingly fair but without emotion. Remi supposed she had to distance herself and keep a clear head. Suddenly her stomach roiled with anxiety and she reached for Paxton's hand to steady herself.

He squeezed it. "Stay calm."

Her stomach eased a little.

"Are your parents coming?"

"No. I told them I would call when it was over."

It seemed like forever before Annie's name was

called. Remi and Paxton walked with Ms. Baxter to stand before the judge on the left. Jim and Kelly Wallace stood on the right with their attorney. Ms. Connors was also there in case the judge wanted to ask questions, Ms. Baxter had said.

"This has been a very difficult decision," the judge said. "Annie is a lucky little girl to have two families who want her. But, sadly, only one can raise her. In light of all the information provided by CPS and upon their recommendation, I'm awarding permanent custody of minor child, Anne Neal, to Jim and Kelly Wallace."

"I'm sorry, Remi," Ms. Baxter said. "We can appeal."

Paxton's arm went around her waist and she stood numb, unable to believe the judge's words.

No! No! No!

Her stomach cramped into a hard ball and she had difficulty breathing. *They'd given Annie to someone else.* Tears welled up at the backs of her eyes and her right hand curled into a fist. She wanted to strike Ms. Baxter, but her hand remained by her side. She wanted to scream and say how unfair it was, but she did none of those things. Paxton's arm tightened around her waist and a calmness came over her. A shaky breath escaped her throat.

"May I see her one last time?" she asked, and she didn't recognize her own voice. She prayed she could get through this without breaking down. There was no way she would cry in the courtroom in front of everyone.

Ms. Baxter turned to face the judge. "My client has a right to say goodbye."

"So ordered," the judge decreed.

Remi, Paxton and Ms. Baxter followed Ms. Connors

down the hall to a small room where Annie was waiting to go home with her new parents. A sob caught in her throat.

Annie lay in a carrier, kicking out with her feet and hands. Her hair was blond like her mother's and her green eyes she'd inherited from her daddy. Remi wondered if she would ever know those things. Annie smiled when she saw Remi and once again tears stung the backs of her eyes. She gritted her teeth and lifted Annie from the carrier.

"Hi, precious." Remi sat in a chair, and Annie laid her head on Remi's shoulder for a moment.

Paxton squatted beside them, and Annie raised her head to look at him. He tickled her stomach and she let out a low giggle. "Hi, little angel." Annie waved a hand at him. "I think she remembers me."

"I think she does, too." Remi held her a little tighter because she had to say something that was going to hurt. Not Annie, but her. "You're going to a new home and you'll have a new mommy and daddy." Remi kissed her cheek and placed a hand on Annie's stomach. "But in your little heart I hope you will have a memory of someone who loved you dearly." She stood up with Annie in her arms and placed her back in the carrier. Ms. Connors watched but she didn't say a word. Remi wanted to say so many things, but she kissed Annie one more time and walked over to where the Wallaces were standing.

"I have some things of her mother's and father's Annie might like when she gets older."

The dark-haired woman replied, "Thank you, that's so nice of you. But Annie is our daughter now and we're starting fresh without memories from the past. We're thinking of changing her name, too."

"What? Her mother gave her that name." Anger boiled through Remi, but she held her tongue.

The woman stiffened. "I'm her mother now."

Paxton took her arm and led her from the room. Ms. Connors stood near the door and Paxton paused to speak to her. Remi kept walking. She couldn't even speak to the woman, but she could hear Paxton's words. "You made a mistake, lady. Have you spent any time with that couple in there? If you had, you would've seen that the woman is wound so tight she's about to fly out of the room and the man is stiff. Have you seen him smile?"

"I beg your pardon."

"Keep begging, lady. I'm telling you you've made the wrong recommendation."

Their words trailed away, and Remi sat in a chair at the end of the hall near glass windows looking out onto the busy Houston traffic. It was all a blur, though, as her world came crashing down around her. The pain shot through her like a million tiny needles, piercing, throbbing, aching until there was nothing left but pain—deep searing pain. She wrapped her arms around her waist to stop the assault. Her fairy tale had disappeared in a cloud of dust. It filled her nostrils with regrets. All the pretending, the lovemaking and the joy of knowing Paxton was over, too. She had to let him go.

Paxton slid into the chair next to her and wrapped his arms around her. "Are you okay?"

"I'm getting there."

"I'm so sorry."

"I know," she said, and looked at his beautiful face. He was her fantasy. Her dream guy. Her fantasy had come true for a few months, and it had been all a dream—a beautiful dream.

"I know it hurts. I'm hurting, too, but we can get through this together. Later, we'll get married and adopt a house full of kids and you'll love them just as much, and this pain will be a vague memory."

Her stomach cramped again and she swallowed hard to say the words she had to. "No. That will never happen."

He drew back, confused. "Why not?"

The truth. The truth. There was nothing so cruel as the truth.

She drew a deep breath. "Annie was my last hope— the child of my heart. I kept believing that love was all we needed. I was a fool."

"Remi…"

She shifted to look at him. "Don't say that my inability to have children doesn't matter."

"Let's talk about it."

She shook her head and it took every ounce of courage she had to say the next words. "There's nothing to talk about. Whatever we had is over."

His eyes narrowed in disbelief. "Come on, Remi. You don't mean that. Our love is about more than Annie."

"One day you'll want kids of your own. Maybe not today, but in the years ahead you'll see your brothers and their families and you'll want what they have. Trust me, every man wants a family."

He cupped her face with his hands, and she wanted to give in, to accept everything he was offering. "I love you and I want a life with you. Why can't you understand that? A child doesn't matter, but if you decide we need a child, we can adopt. We can have a child, Remi."

"But you can have your own and I'm not taking that from you. I love you too much to do that. You deserve everything that life offers. I'm broken and there's no way to fix me. I—"

"To me you're not broken. You're my love. My one and only love. Remember I said at your apartment that whatever happened we would still love each other. We would still have a future."

Her strength was waning and it took an effort to respond. "I let myself dream that with Annie our lives would be perfect, and not being able to have a child wouldn't matter. We would have Annie. But it does matter. It matters a great deal." She reached in her purse and pulled out her key ring. Removing a key, she added, "This is my apartment key so you can remove your things. It's over. It really is over. We should have never gotten involved in the first place. There were too many obstacles in our way. All of this is on me. I was weak. I wanted it all, and I apologize for that. Goodbye, Paxton…" She got to her feet, and he grabbed her hand.

"I'll never say goodbye to you. Never."

An errant tear escaped and she brushed it away quickly and handed him the key. He wouldn't take it so she laid it on a chair and walked as fast as she could to the women's bathroom across the hall. She slid down the tiled wall, weak and unable to stand on her own. Her body trembled and she wrapped her arms around her raised knees. It was over. As the impact hit her, she cursed life, the accident and love for ripping her heart out. Then she let the tears she'd been holding in flow freely. She cried for Paxton. She cried for herself. And she cried for the life they would never have.

After a few minutes, she got to her feet and went to the sink to wash her face. She dabbed at her eyes and took a deep breath. She'd lost everything and she wondered what she was supposed to do now. She'd been telling Paxton that she was stronger and now she had to prove it. Walking out of this bathroom and into a new life would be one of the hardest things she would ever have to do. But she was a survivor. If she had learned anything in the past few months, it was that she could go on. Without tears. Maybe a few regrets. But she would go on.

Without Paxton.

Chapter Fourteen

How could she do this? kept running through Paxton's head as he drove to Remi's apartment. She wouldn't even give them a chance. She just said, no, it was over. How could she do that to him? He parked at her apartment and slammed the steering wheel with his hand.

"Damn it!" He sat there for a moment trying to believe that what just happened had happened. As he thought about it, the anger in him subsided. He knew her so well. She was trying to give him what she thought he deserved. A family. A baby. When she lost Annie, all her defenses went back up. Everything depended on Annie—her life, her future. Their future.

He could only imagine the pain she went through when they'd told her she would never have children. Today those words were spoken all over again inside her heart. She was shutting everyone out, including him. He couldn't reach her. The only thing he could do now was to give her time. He wasn't giving up on them.

As he went into the apartment, he noticed the baby things on the sofa. And there was the crib and all of Annie's stuff in her bedroom. She didn't need to see that when she came home. He went to the nightstand and found her address book. He called her father and told him what had happened.

"I just thought you might want to take all of the baby things out of her apartment."

"Yes, I'll do that, but first I have to find my daughter and make sure she's okay. I'll take her home to her mother. Thank you, Paxton."

"Just take care of her."

Paxton stared down at the boots in front of him. He was still getting her a pair for her birthday. For sizing, he picked up a pair of black leather boots to take with him. In the living room he grabbed his bag, which he hadn't even unpacked. He took one last look around the apartment where he'd found love and happiness. And now it was over.

It didn't take him long to find a FedEx store to ship a package to Kincaid Boots. There were so many boots in her closet he wondered if she would even miss them. He turned the truck toward I-35 and Oklahoma, leaving everything he loved behind. His dad had always said that big boys and cowboys don't cry. A tear fell onto his shirt. His dad had lied. This hurt. This hurt like hell.

He drove on through the night, stopping only once for gas. It was still dark when he pulled up to the trailer and the rodeo arena parking area. He unlocked the door and went inside. Cole and Dakota were sound asleep on the sofa bed. Walking down the hall, exhaustion pulled at him.

With a long sigh, he removed his hat and placed it on the dresser. His belt and gold buckle followed. He pulled off his boots and fell onto the bed, hoping the darkness would claim him and that when he woke up this would all be a bad dream.

REMI WASN'T DOING WELL, but she would never let it show. Her parents wanted her to come home for a few days, like they always did when Remi had a crisis. Her dad had removed all the baby things from her apartment and she was grateful for that. But this time she had to handle the crisis alone because she had caused it. Every night she cried herself to sleep, holding Paxton's pillow. She had to get a grip and soon, or depression would claim her. Annie was lost to her forever. And so was Paxton. She had to accept that.

Her mornings were busy with therapy, but the afternoons were lonely and she needed to find something to do during that time. She bought a bicycle and rode it around the city's trails for hours. Her legs were getting stronger and stronger.

Her dad stopped by one day, which was unexpected since she'd told her parents that she would call if she needed them. They sat in the living room.

"You look good," her dad said.

"I bought a bike and I've been riding it all over Houston."

"Now, sweetheart, I don't mean to interfere, but be careful where you go."

"Don't worry. I am."

He scooted forward on the sofa. "I came over here with a suggestion and, once again, I don't mean to interfere in your life. I just think you need something to occupy your time."

She wasn't annoyed because she knew her parents loved her. She just hoped the suggestion wasn't to call Paxton. "What is it?"

"We have so many elderly patients in the hospital who come from nursing homes around Houston with a broken hip or knee or arm or something and they have no family to visit them. Usually their children live far away or just don't care. We have volunteers to help with this and I was hoping that you might like to volunteer. It's easy. You just go into the room and ask if they need anything. Some elderly people just like to talk, others like to be read to and others just like to see a smiling face. The hospital tries to do all they can to cheer them up because it helps in their recovery."

Remi couldn't imagine anyone not visiting their grandparents in the hospital. She talked to Gran almost every day and she would continue to do so. She planned to go on the weekend to see her and her parents were going, too, but in separate vehicles. Remi planned to stay a little longer.

"I'd like that, but I can only work in the afternoons."

"No problem. Just come over to the hospital and I'll introduce you to Barbara Sayers. You can pick your hours."

She smiled at her father. "Now will you stop worrying about me? I'm fine, Dad. Really." And Paxton would bite her finger if he was here. When would she stop thinking about him?

"You loved him so much. Your mother and I worry."

"I know. And now I'll be busier than ever."

Her dad rubbed his hands together and she knew he was fighting to hold words in. "You know, sweetheart, it doesn't matter to some men—"

"Dad, we're not having this discussion." She stopped him before he could go any further. No one understood her decision, including Gran. But she had to give Paxton a chance to find someone else. It was the right thing to do. She kept telling herself that day after day.

Her dad left, and Remi was once again alone in an apartment that had Paxton's memory everywhere. She could move to another apartment, but that wouldn't solve the problem. Paxton was in her heart and always would be. She had to cowboy-up, as she'd heard Paxton say, and keep busy and keep going. That was all she could do now.

IN OKLAHOMA PAXTON couldn't get Remi out of his mind and it was throwing him off his game. When he rode bulls, he could shut out the world. But he couldn't shut out her face. It was right there, every time. And he found himself eating dirt instead of staying on the bull eight seconds. It happened three times and he couldn't seem to hit his stride. The younger guys were kicking his butt.

As they moved on to Jasper, Texas, Paxton knew his friends wanted to say something, but they kept quiet. As they got ready to go to the arena, they broke the silence.

Cole scratched his head. "Pax, you've dropped out of the standings with your performance last night. You have to get her out of your head or you're going to lose the whole season. As a friend, I'm telling you, you have to do something."

"Yeah, Pax, don't let a girl ruin your season," Dakota added.

He'd told his friends about what had happened, and they cared about him, but he wished they'd stay out of his business. He had screwed up and he already knew that. A reminder he didn't need.

"I'm working on it," he replied. "Now let's go over to the arena."

Just then the door of the trailer opened and Phoenix

and Elias stepped in. Cole and Dakota slithered out the door like two backstabbing rattlesnakes.

"What are y'all doing here?"

Opening the small refrigerator, Elias asked, "Got any beer?" He pulled out a can before Paxton could reply and popped the top.

"We're not here for beer, Elias," Phoenix said, taking a seat on the sofa. Elias joined him, and Paxton stared at his two brothers. He knew why they were here. He was blowing his career, and they had something to say about it.

"Why are y'all here?" Paxton asked anyway.

"I'm sorry about what happened," Phoenix said. "Miss Bertie told Mom and I know how much you loved Remi. But you can't let this ruin your career."

"Yeah." Elias joined the conversation. "I work my butt off on the ranch doing your share of the work and when you don't win money that means no money is coming into the ranch account. Nada. Nothing."

Phoenix frowned at Elias. "Just let me do the talking."

Elias shrugged. "Just saying."

Paxton sat in the table booth. "You don't have to tell me that, Elias. I'm smart enough to figure that one out myself."

Phoenix twirled his hat in his hands. "You were with me when I went through all that angst with Rosie. She let the Rebel/McCray feud come between us and said we could never be happy. I loved her and I wasn't going to give up. I waited and waited. You sat with me in the chapel as I waited. Remember?"

Paxton nodded, remembering his brother's pain.

"That's what you have to do now. Give her time and

she'll come around. In the meantime you need to do some thinking about what you want. Do you want children? You never seemed that fond of them."

"I wanted that little girl just as much as she did," he said without pausing. "I want Remi to understand that I'm hurting, too, but I can't get through to her."

"That's what time is for, Pax." Phoenix studied his hat. "You know, you were really down after the finals last year. You were upset about what had happened with Jenny and Lisa and you didn't feel good about yourself, so you and Elias drank yourselves silly. Didn't solve anything. You were still conflicted about your future. You took some time off in January to get your mind clear and then you met Remi and you changed overnight. None of us recognized you, helping Miss Bertie and being an all-around good guy." Phoenix raised his eyes to Paxton's. "Now don't get angry, but I think Remi is your redemption."

He wasn't angry. He already knew. Tapping his fingers on the table, he replied, "You're right. She is my redemption. She makes me a better person. A better man."

"Ye gads," Elias muttered. "I'm gonna barf in my beer. Cowboys don't talk like that. What's happened to you?"

"It's called love," Phoenix told Elias. "You just wait. Your day is coming and Paxton and I are going to laugh and laugh and laugh our heads off."

Elias shook his head. "It'll never happen. I'll never let a woman have that much control over me."

"Just be quiet, Elias." Phoenix turned back to Paxton. "I don't know if I told you, but Rosie might not be able to conceive another child because her ex beat her so bad and she had a lot of internal injuries, and an ovary removed. I told her if we can't get pregnant, then we'll adopt. Did you mention adopting again to Remi?"

"I did, and she said I could have my own and she wouldn't take that away from me. She wouldn't listen to anything I had to say."

"A true McCray," Elias murmured under his breath.

Paxton jumped to his feet and pointed a finger at Elias. "Don't you say a word about Remi or I'll put your lights out."

Elias placed his beer on the floor and stood slowly, his eyes trained on Paxton. His brother was tall and muscled but that didn't bother Paxton. He'd take him on any day of the week, especially if he said one more thing about Remi.

Elias poked a finger into Paxton's chest. "You're gonna put my lights out?"

"Stop this," Phoenix intervened, but his brothers weren't listening.

"Yeah," Paxton replied.

Elias got up in Paxton's face. "Come on, then."

Before Paxton knew it, his right fist connected with Elias's jaw and Elias went flying backward onto the sofa, knocking Phoenix's hat to the floor. He was winded only for a second before he bolted up and came after Paxton. He charged like a bull and they went flying backward into the bedroom. The trailer shook from the assault. They flipped over the bed and landed between the bed and the wall, which was a very small space. Elias was on the bottom and Paxton was on top. He rolled to the bed and reached out his arm to Elias, who he pulled onto the bed with him.

Elias rubbed his jaw. "I think you broke it. Who knew you were that strong?"

"You knocked the breath out of me." Paxton sucked air into his lungs and then all of a sudden he started laughing.

"What's so funny?" Phoenix asked from the doorway.

"We're fighting like kids, like we used to do on the ranch. But we're adults now and we need to start acting like it."

Phoenix looked at Elias. "I don't think he's ever going to make the transformation. Fighting is in his blood."

"Hey." Elias was still nursing his jaw. "A good fight gets rid of a lot of tension."

Paxton scooted to sit on the side of the bed. "You know, he's right. I had this ball right here—" he put his hand on his heart "—it was pressing into my chest and sometimes I found it hard to breathe. But now, it's gone." He took a long breath. "Remi wouldn't want me to throw my career away. I have to ride for her. I can focus now. I got it under control. Thanks, brothers."

Elias sat up. "Brothers? Phoenix didn't do a thing."

"Give it a rest, Elias," Phoenix said.

Paxton and Elias stood up, face-to-face, and without either of them thinking about it, they hugged. His family had his back when he was down and when he was up. There was nothing like family.

REMI WAS BUSIER than ever volunteering at the hospital. It took up a lot of her time and she found she enjoyed it. The elderly were much like children, but they tended to be grouchy, rude and opinionated.

Mrs. Dixon was ninety years old and she had smoked all her life. She had two children who lived up north and she rarely saw them. Diagnosed with lung cancer, she refused to let the doctors operate on her. She was on oxygen and spent most of her days begging for cigarettes.

Remi knocked on the door and went into the room.

Mrs. Dixon sat up in bed, oxygen tubing in her nose. "You got a cigarette, dearie?" She talked with a wheeze.

"You know you can't have a cigarette. You're on oxygen."

"The lady at the home always brought me one. She'd take me outside and let me smoke. I don't know why you can't do the same. A young thing like you can get a cigarette off anybody."

The lady was persistent and she didn't know quite how to explain it to her any other way, but she thought she might have a solution to the problem. She reached into her pink jacket and pulled out some nicotine gum. "This gum has nicotine in it and you might enjoy chewing it. It might offer you some relief. The nurse said you still have your own teeth so it shouldn't be too hard." She checked with the nurse always before she offered the patients anything.

"Gum? I want a cigarette. If you don't have one, then get out of my room."

Remi laid the gum on the nightstand and walked out. Some days were like that, but others were very rewarding. She went down the hall to Mr. Schaeffer's room. He was eighty-eight years old and had broken his ankle. His room was always full of family and kids. Today two of his daughters and their grown children were in the room.

"Good afternoon," Remi said. "I just dropped by to give Mr. Schaeffer the TV schedule for the hospital TV. He asked for it this morning."

"Thank you," Mr. Schaeffer said, taking the paper from her.

"That's so sweet," one of the daughters said. She hugged her dad. "I think they're spoiling you here." There were quick hugs and kisses and suddenly the room emptied.

Mr. Schaeffer scooted up in the bed. "It's like a whirlwind. That's what my wife used to say. They come and then they're gone."

"But it's nice to have such a big family." Remi looked at all the family photos on his nightstand.

"Yeah. But it's not the same without my wife."

"I'm sorry." Then she told him about her gran and her grandpa and he listened avidly. He talked about the olden times and how hard it was and she listened with an open heart and open mind. He really just wanted someone to listen, like most older people.

Her last visit for the day was with Mrs. Ashbury. She'd fallen and broken her hip. She didn't come from one of the nursing homes, Barbara had said. She wanted Remi to check in with the woman because her husband was becoming a nuisance to the nurses.

She knocked on the door and went in. An elderly distinguished-looking gentleman stood on the far side of the bed, but as soon as he saw Remi he quickly came to the other side, blocking Remi from his wife.

"Can I help you, dear?" he asked.

"I'm Remi Roberts and I'm a volunteer here at the hospital. I came to see if Mrs. Ashbury needed anything."

The man shook his snow-white head. "No, she doesn't need anything. I'm always here to take care of her."

Remi saw something move beneath the blanket and sheet. It traveled from the foot of the bed up to Mrs. Ashbury, who Remi still couldn't see.

"Give it up, Alfred," the woman in the bed said. "I think she already knows."

Mr. Ashbury stepped aside, and Remi saw a white poodle's head poking out from the sheet, curled into Mrs. Ashbury.

"This is Baby," Mrs. Ashbury said. "She misses me so Alfred brings her to visit and we're afraid the nurses might object." The woman wore a lacy pink bed jacket and diamonds flashed on her fingers. Usually the hospital requested that all jewelry be removed. The lady was as distinguished as her husband.

Remi reached over and petted the dog's head. "I have a dog and her name is Sadie."

"I'm going home tomorrow so the nurses shouldn't mind, should they?"

Remi was going to leave that up to the nurses. For no reason would she tell them they couldn't keep their dog in the room. That was just her opinion. "I'll talk to them."

The man took a seat. "Are you in high school? Do you volunteer when you're out of class?"

Good heavens! Did she look that young?

"I've been out of high school for a long time. I'm a pre-K teacher."

"Isn't that nice, Alfred?"

"Yes, Maude. That's real nice. Wish they had teachers like her when I was in school."

"Alfred!" She turned to Remi. "He's a cad. He always has been."

"How long have you been married?"

"Sixty-two years."

"Oh, how wonderful. Congratulations! Not many people stay together that long."

Alfred got up and came to the bed and took Maude's hand. "It's been a good life."

"How many children do you have?"

"None," Mrs. Ashbury replied. "It's always been just me and Alfred."

Remi didn't want to appear nosy, but she had to ask. "Did you want children?"

Mrs. Ashbury stroked Alfred's hand. "In the beginning we thought we might have a child, but then we found out Alfred has a low sperm count. He offered me a divorce and I told him where he could stick that. I loved him too much and I would never give him up. He's a retired colonel in the army and we've traveled all over the world. I couldn't have done that with children. Today we're content. We have no regrets." She glanced at her husband. "Right, honey?"

"Right."

The poodle whimpered and Mrs. Ashbury lifted the dog into the crook of her arm. Remi soon left, but the image of the two elderly lovebirds stuck with her for some time. She didn't cry herself to sleep that night. There was nothing left to cry about. She had made a decision and she had to stick to it. But doubts were beginning to leak through her defenses.

PAXTON GOT HIS rhythm back and no one was happier about it than him. But he was still behind in the national standings. Barron was at the top and then Goodready, Haaz and Hightower. Barron was already projected to win in Vegas. Paxton still had some fight left in him and he was going to make it very hard for the kid. Since the young guys were at the top of the standings, the announcers were billing them as the young kids against the old guys. Paxton had a lot to prove.

During June, July and August they were into the heavy rodeo season. They'd crisscrossed the country to catch every important rodeo to build their points. Remi's birthday was coming up and he wanted to go home for that and he didn't know why. She didn't want to see him.

He was dog tired some days and other days he just didn't care. The rodeo took all of his energy and that was the way he wanted it. At night he fell into a dead sleep, but her image was right there torturing him, even with the darkness surrounding him.

Chapter Fifteen

In June it was Remi's birthday and she wanted to spend it in Horseshoe with her grandmother. She went a day early to help Gran. Paxton's memory was everywhere, but she was better equipped to deal with it now. It still hurt, but she was clinging to her decision with every ounce of strength in her.

In the afternoon she went over and visited Rosie. They talked on the patio while Jake and Dixie, Rosie's dog, played in a small swimming pool Rosie had bought at Walmart. She was babysitting John, Falcon's son, and the two boys were splashing around yelling and having fun with the dog. They talked about family and kids. Rosie didn't mention Paxton and neither did Remi. It was one subject she didn't want to talk about.

On Saturday her parents came and Ruger did, too. Gran had made a feast, including strawberry short-cake, Remi's favorite. It was a family day and everyone seemed to enjoy it, even her brother. They were talking at the kitchen table when someone knocked at the door.

Remi stood up. "I'll get it."

She opened the door to a FedEx man. "I have a package for Ms. Remi Roberts."

"That's me."

He stuck out a gadget for her to sign. Who was it from? She couldn't think of anyone who would send her something at her grandmother's. The family came into the living room to see what was going on.

Ruger brought the box inside and placed it in the middle of the floor. "It's from Kincaid Boots," he announced.

Boots! Only one person would send her boots.

Paxton.

Ruger took out his pocket knife and ripped open the box. Remi knelt down and with a shaky hand she lifted the lid. There were three boxes inside. She pulled out the first one and opened it. Inside was a pair of black leather boots with no more than a half inch heel. They were gorgeous and soft and had a zipper up the side for easy access. She ran her hand over the smooth leather and a sob caught in her throat.

She swallowed hard and pulled out the second box, which were camel-colored boots with filigree up the side. They were gorgeous. Hardly breathing, she pulled out the third box. Inside was a pair of cowgirl boots. The most beautiful boots she'd ever seen. The top was turquoise and glittered with rhinestones. The foot part was a light brown with turquoise filigree on the side. She held them to her chest. She liked them the most because they reminded her of him.

No one asked who the boots were from. She gathered them up and carried them to her room. Sitting on the side of the bed, she tried to figure out what to do. Should she thank him? Or just let it go? Or maybe she should send them back. Everything in her screamed no. She wouldn't hurt him that way again.

She reached for her phone and touched his name.

She sent a simple text: Thank you! Then she put on her cowgirl boots and walked into the living room. They fit perfectly and didn't hurt her feet. How did he know her size? Her black boots were missing and she'd thought she had probably taken them to the nurses by mistake. But she had a sneaky idea that Paxton had taken them.

She twirled around in the living room. "What do y'all think?"

"I think Handsome has good taste," her grandmother replied.

"Are you okay, sweetheart?" her mother asked.

"I don't know," she answered honestly. "I feel like a leaf floating on water and I don't know which way I'm going to go. Other forces seem to be guiding me."

"Oh, sweetheart." Her dad wrapped his arms around her, and she felt safe and secure once again. But she was an adult now and she needed more. She just didn't know how to make it work with a clear conscience. Standing in her beautiful cowgirl boots, her mind drifted with thoughts of fairy tales and happy endings. Maybe, like Mrs. Ashbury, having a child didn't matter to Paxton. Maybe love was all they needed.

Could that be possible?

PAXTON LAY IN bed resting for the rodeo tonight. Keeping up with the younger guys was taking a toll on all of them. Cole and Dakota were asleep also. His phone binged and he rolled over to see who it was. *Remi!* He jumped up and grabbed his phone, but it was only a text. Thank you! She'd gotten the boots. Why couldn't she call him? Why couldn't she at least have called him?

Frustrated, he slammed the phone on the nightstand. So many thoughts ran through his mind, but he had to do what Phoenix had said. He had to wait on her to make the right decision. He now knew what his brother had gone through all those months ago. He never dreamed he could hurt like this.

Unable to resist, he reached for his phone and looked at all the pictures of Annie that Remi had sent him. He had been resisting doing this, but now he let the pain rip through him. Annie should be theirs. He went to sleep with a photo of Remi on his phone clutched tight in his hand.

As ALWAYS, HE threw himself into the rodeo. They were either driving to a rodeo or they were at a rodeo. There was no time to go home or time to do anything else. The focus was on rodeo and Vegas. They closed out July with Cheyenne Frontier Days. He beat Barron on the last day and that did a lot for his confidence and his goals for Vegas. Barron had been unlucky and had drawn the bull Misfit. Paxton hadn't ridden him yet, but he was known to be brutal. Everyone knew the bull was going to be bull of the year and Paxton was hoping to get a chance to ride him before Vegas. Turn It On was another bull known to buck cowboys into the dirt. Top-Notch was another that wreaked havoc. Everyone was at the top of their game and so were the bulls.

July faded into August and the cowboys were getting injured. Paxton hurt his arm in Cheyenne, but with a little ice it was as good as new. Cole broke his finger and Dakota hit his head on a fence, but they were back the next night to ride. That was the way cowboys were. They were always ready.

When the season ended, Paxton relaxed. He'd made the top fifteen, which had been his goal. Barron was still at the top of the standings with Paxton second. Goodready was third followed by Hightower, Cole, Haaz and Dakota. More cowboys followed. They were all headed for Vegas.

Paxton's bones ached and his chest hurt so he went home to rest for a few days. He had made a lot of money this season so he didn't feel guilty about not working. But once he was home he couldn't sit around. He helped Elias build a fence on some land he had cleared. Later he thought of going to see Miss Bertie, but Remi might be there and he had to wait. The waiting was killing him.

September arrived with cooler temperatures and Paxton and his friends hit the circuit again to stay fresh. They were all addicted to the ride. This would be his last season. He was getting older and his body couldn't take it anymore. That was a hard pill to swallow, but sometimes a man had to admit the truth.

He had Thanksgiving with the family and he and his friends flew out to Vegas for the big show. As always, it was a lot of excitement and flash and glitter and anything else you wanted to see. They got in early to rest and to stay focused. His friends went out drinking and to party. They begged Paxton to go, but that part of his life was over and he had no interest in spending most of the night in a bar with some girl he had never met before hanging on him. He stayed in his room and watched television, wondering where Remi was and if she was thinking of him.

IN AUGUST, REMI went back to teaching and a lot of things changed in her life. She didn't have time to volunteer at the hospital anymore and she ended her therapy sessions. She had achieved all of her goals and she was healthy again. Her time now was filled with fresh faces, trusting eyes and hearts full of love. She would miss her elderly patients. A nurse had called and said that Mrs. Dixon had passed away. Remi was sad for a few days, but she knew wherever Mrs. Dixon was she now had a cigarette.

She was busy and the days passed quickly. Soon Thanksgiving arrived and the family planned to spend it at Gran's because Ruger wouldn't come to Houston. Gran mentioned that Paxton was home for Thanksgiving, as if to nudge her. He was just a few miles away and she was tempted, but she held fast.

The National Finals Rodeo was coming up and Remi packed her things and headed for Gran's. It was the end of the first week in December and they were going to watch the start of the rodeo together. She was so excited that Paxton had made it and she was going to watch every second. She didn't analyze why it was so important to her. She just had to do it. The show started with a bang and a lot of talk about the younger guys against the older guys.

Who were they calling old?

She saw Paxton as he rode out with the other participants of the rodeo. Cole and Dakota were beside him. "To the left are his friends he travels with," she pointed out to Gran.

The camera zeroed in on Paxton and the announcer said it was going to be a dogfight between Paxton and Barron Flynn. The announcers talked back and forth and questioned how much juice Paxton had left in the tank. He'd been rodeoing for years and they wondered if this would be his last season.

She wondered that, too.

It seemed like forever before the bull riding came on. It was the last event and Remi's eyes were glued to the screen. Paxton was the second to last to ride. She held her breath as he slid onto the bull. Paxton appeared strong, vital and all male. Her heart beat a little faster at the thought. Phoenix was on the chute talking to him and helping him with the bull rope. Cole was on the other side. It amazed her that the cowboys competed against each other yet supported one another when they rode. She guessed it was the cowboy way. When Paxton scored a ninety, she jumped up and shouted.

Gran glanced at her. "Have you asked yourself why you're so excited about Handsome riding?"

"Don't start, Gran." Remi resumed her seat and waited for Barron Flynn to ride. She hadn't watched Paxton ride all season because it would've been too painful. She was giving him a chance, was the way she looked at it, but as each day passed she was more conflicted than ever. It had been months and she wondered if he was seeing other girls. She didn't really want to know the answer.

Barron scored an eighty-nine, and Remi stood and cheered again. Gran gave her a sideways look. Paxton won the night and she was happy for him. But the second night Barron won and Remi had to wonder how long Paxton could keep up the pace with the young kid. But her money was on Paxton all the way.

Sunday night she packed her things and headed back to Houston. She had to teach the next day, but every night during the week she was glued to the TV and she could see what the announcers were talking about. Paxton and Barron were trading wins back and forth. A guy named Goodready was in there and so were Cole and Dakota. But the dogfight was between Paxton and Barron. Paxton had won three nights and so had Barron. They were neck and neck going into the last two days.

On Thursday school let out for the holidays and Remi went back to Gran's to watch the final two nights. Brady Haaz won and it all came down to Saturday. Who was going to walk away with the title? The announcers were upping the tension. It would either be Paxton or Barron and Remi could hardly wait. For the first time she thought about Paxton losing and her heart ached. She didn't want him to lose. She wanted him to always win. That was a sobering thought.

The next morning Remi walked out to the pond to watch Henry and Henny. They sat on the bank squawking at each other. She was sure they had a language all their own. Several other geese were on the other side of the pond, but Henry and Henny ignored them. Henny pecked in the dry, brittle grass and seemed oblivious to the forty-degree temperature. Suddenly, Henny stood up and flapped her one good wing. Henry did the same. Henny sank to the grass and Henry followed. He was always there with her. Always.

Remi huddled in her jacket trying to come to grips with everything she was feeling. She loved Paxton; there was no doubt about that. Could they have a life together? Could they have a happy life?

Henny squawked at Henry and Remi stared at the male goose. "Why do you stay here? You can fly. You can be with other geese, but yet you stay with Henny and her broken wing. Why don't you fly away, Henry?" The goose stood and flapped his wings in an aggressive manner. The other geese were swimming toward them and Henry was on guard.

Why don't you fly away, Henry? Then it hit her. They mated for life. They were soul mates, just like her and Paxton. Henry didn't want to fly away because that meant he would have to leave Henny. She was his love. His only love.

Paxton had said the same words to her.

She got up and hurried toward the house, Sadie at her heels. She stopped at the oak tree and remembered the day Paxton had made her the cane. He'd loved her when she'd been pale and thin. He'd loved her all scarred and broken. He'd loved her unconditionally.

How could she have been so blind?

SATURDAY NIGHT ARRIVED faster than Paxton had really wanted. His body was tired and his bones ached but tonight would be the most important night of his life. Almost. Without Remi, it didn't mean too much. But he'd worked hard for this and he planned to go out a winner. There was one problem, though. He'd drawn the bull Misfit, the bull only a couple of cowboys had ridden all season. How could his luck be so bad?

Paxton sat in the locker room putting on his chaps and spurs. Phoenix was there, too. Only personnel and cowboys were allowed in the cowboy area, but everyone knew Phoenix and no one said a thing.

"You have to focus, Pax." Phoenix had been preaching to him about an hour and Paxton was growing tired of it.

"Give it a rest," Paxton said. "I know what I have to do."

"I don't think you do. You look like your dog died or something. You seem to be somewhere else."

Paxton stood and straightened his chaps. "I just wish she was here. It would mean so much more if Remi was here."

"Don't you think she's watching?"

"What?" He never thought of her watching the rodeo. When she said it was over, he assumed that was it. "Do you think she's watching?"

"Uh, um, sure." There was something in Phoenix's voice, and Paxton knew he was lying.

"You're lying."

Phoenix stood. "Okay. Remi's watching."

"How do you know that?"

"From Rosie."

Three little words—*Remi is watching*—lifted his spirits and riding Misfit became more important than ever. He had to ride for her and his confidence was high. He just had to focus, as Phoenix had said. Grabbing his duffel bag out of his locker, a small smile played with the corners of his mouth. Oh, yeah, he could do this. He turned and came face-to-face with Barron.

An arrogant grin stretched across the kid's face. "You might as well bow out of this one, old man. That title is mine."

"You better learn…" Paxton put up a hand to stop Phoenix.

"Actions speak louder than words, kid." He walked out with Phoenix behind him, feeling ten feet tall and bulletproof.

It was time for the last event of the night—bull riding. The Thomas and Mack Center in Las Vegas, Nevada, was packed with eager fans shouting and yelling, but Paxton didn't look. He hated seeing all the girls with Heartthrob and Paxton on their T-shirts. His whole family and Jericho were here for the big event. Later, they planned a big celebration, win or lose.

Phoenix stood beside him as they watched the first bull rider take a nosedive into the dirt. Barron was standing six feet away from Paxton. But he made no move to speak to him again, which was just as well. Cole and Dakota flanked Paxton on the other side. Before Cole had to ride, the highest score was eighty-five. Paxton walked with Cole to the chute to help him get ready. His mind now was totally on the rodeo.

Cole scored an eighty-seven and next was Dakota, who scored an eighty-eight. Goodready was next and Paxton watched along with his friends to see what the young man could do at his first National Finals Rodeo. He'd drawn the bull Turn It Up. It was a good ride and everyone waited for the score. Eighty-nine popped up—the highest score of the night. Goodready had set the bar high. Paxton was next. He took a deep breath and walked to the chute.

Cole and Dakota were on one side and Phoenix on the other as they adjusted Paxton's bull rope around Misfit's chest. He didn't want to hear any more advice. He just wanted to ride. But Misfit was shaking the chute trying to get out. They waited for him to calm down and then Paxton slid onto the bull's back. Misfit began to struggle again. Paxton had to get off as the handlers tried to calm him once again. It was putting a strain on his focus.

Once again he got the signal and slid onto the bull. Beneath him, he felt the power of eighteen hundred pounds of muscle and strength. The speckle white bull with sawed-off horns stank of rawhide, sweat and manure. Paxton was used to that, though. Bulls did not smell like a rose garden. The bull twisted his head agitatedly and snot dripped off the steel bars of the chute. Paxton worked his rosined gloved hand into the handle of his bull rope, flexing his fingers and testing his strength.

"You got it, Pax," Cole said.

"Just stay focused," Dakota added.

Paxton didn't reply. He was shutting everything out. Everything but Misfit.

"Ready?" Phoenix asked.

This time Paxton raised his left arm and nodded. The gate swung open and Misfit reared up on his back legs and vaulted into the arena like a wild bronc. Kicking out with his back legs, the bull went into a spin and then changed directions. Paxton's head was spinning but he held on, maintaining his position. Just when he thought he couldn't hold on one second longer, he heard the buzz. Eight seconds. Done. He leaped from the bull, turned a flip and managed to get to his feet. The bullfighters quickly got him out of the way of Misfit, who was charging toward them. Paxton jumped over the fence, safe.

Leaning on the arena railing, he sucked air into his tight lungs. He'd done it. He'd ridden Misfit. The world seeped back into his mind and he could hear the announcers.

"What do you think, Hal?"

"I think that's the ride of Paxton Rebel's life. He gave it everything he had and he's waiting to see if the judges think the same thing. The Rebel family is here and Paxton Rebel fans are everywhere with their pink

T-shirts and Heartthrob on them. A lot of young girls are cheering for Paxton. The noise in here is deafening."

"Yeah, Bob. Everyone's on their feet as they wait for the score. But no one wants to see that score more than Paxton."

The announcer was right about that. Paxton kept waiting. He was good at waiting. Phoenix, Cole and Dakota joined him, slapping him on the back.

"What a ride!" Phoenix beamed with pride for his brother.

"Man, I don't think Barron can beat you now," Cole said.

"It has to be a high score," Dakota added.

Paxton was hoping the same thing but still there was no score on the scoreboard. What was taking so long? He could hear the announcers asking the same question. Then all of a sudden it was there. Ninety-one. There was nothing to celebrate because there was one rider left. Barron.

He'd drawn the bull Top-Notch. The voices and the people around Paxton faded as he watched Barron Flynn try to beat him. This was it. It was excruciating to watch. His whole career came down to this.

Top-Notch bucked, twisted and tried to dislodge Barron to no avail. He rode the bull like a professional, as he had all season. Now Paxton had to wait again. It was going to be close, even he knew that. Neither his friends nor Phoenix spoke. It was a tense moment as everyone's eyes were on the scoreboard. Everyone in the Thomas and Mack Center were on their feet. Waiting.

Paxton stomach curled into a ball of tension. Cameras were everywhere and he was sure he was on the big screen because they were focused on him most of the time. They wanted to get his reaction when the score came up. He wouldn't react. He would just walk away to the locker room.

The cheering and the voices stopped. The Thomas and Mack Center became very quiet as some people bit their nails and waited for the score. The wait was getting to Paxton, but he would not show one sign of weakness. He would be a professional to the end. He didn't know where Barron was, but he was going to shake his hand one way or another.

Phoenix put his arm around Paxton's shoulders. "Relax. You got this one."

He heard the cheering before he saw the score. Ninety. Paxton sucked in a breath of relief. He'd won. Cowboys crowded around him, shaking his hand, hugging him. A microphone was stuck in his face and he answered questions and he hadn't a clue of what he was saying. There seemed to be a whirlwind taking him down. But this would be a moment he would remember forever.

Barron stood to the side, his face a mask of disappointment. Paxton walked up to him and held out his hand. "It was a good ride."

"Thanks, man, I almost had you."

"Next year it's all yours."

Another microphone was stuck in his face and he answered more questions.

Phoenix pulled him aside. "Smile, for heaven's sake, or you're going to break their cameras."

"It would have meant so much more if Remi was here."

"Jake is waving at you. Look up in the stands where the family is sitting and wave back."

He wouldn't disappoint Jake so he looked where his family was standing. Someone was holding Jake and it wasn't Rosie. Jake had a hat on so he couldn't see the person's face, but then Rosie took Jake and he saw her. *Remi. She was here.* His heart soared and for a moment he wasn't sure what to do. A phone buzzed and Phoenix held up Paxton's phone, which Paxton had given him before the ride. He yanked it away from Phoenix and saw it was Remi.

With a shaky hand, he touched her name.

"How do I get to you?" Remi asked.

"Just go left out of the stands and I'll meet you."

He took a moment to look at his brother. "You knew she was here and you didn't tell me."

Phoenix shrugged. "She wouldn't let me. She didn't want to ruin your focus and I agreed with her. Are you going to stand here arguing with me or are you going to go meet her?"

Paxton took off running through the crowd with his spurs and chaps still on. People were pulling at him to shake his hand or to get an autograph and the girls were the worst, trying to touch him, but he kept running, shaking off their hands. He stopped when he saw Remi standing in the crowd looking for him.

When he'd first met her, he'd been conflicted about his feelings for her, but he wasn't anymore. He loved her. Her skin glowed and the way she filled out those jeans made his pulse leap. Thick long hair fell past her shoulders. She tucked a strand behind her ear in a nervous gesture he remembered well. His eyes caught the turquoise boots he'd sent her. She was dressed in a cowgirl shirt, too. She was beautiful, just as she was in his dreams.

She turned and spotted him and took off running. He ran to meet her, scooping her up into his arms and swinging her around. She buried her face in his neck.

"I love you," she breathed against his skin.

"I love you, too." He kissed her neck, her cheek, and caught her lips in a searing kiss. Cameras flashed around them but that didn't bother Paxton. They could take all the photos they wanted. He had what he wanted.

Against her lips, he whispered, "Does this mean…?"

"Yes. It means we're planning a wedding."

He leaned his forehead against hers. "What made you change your mind?"

"Henry."

"Henry? You mean the goose?"

She nodded. "I couldn't figure out why he didn't fly away. Why did he stay on the pond with Henny? Then I knew…"

"Because they mated for life," he finished for her.

"Yes. I realized that you and I have a love like that. A forever love."

"God bless Henry." Paxton smiled into her beautiful eyes. "We can do whatever you want. Doesn't matter to me if we have children. But if you want to adopt, I'm with you all the way. But this—" he gathered her into his arms and held her close "—you and I are forever."

"Forever," she murmured before he took her lips once again.

Chapter Sixteen

Life was crazy and Paxton was enjoying every minute of it. After all the festivities in Vegas were over, they flew into Austin where Paxton had his truck and Remi had her SUV in a parking garage. He dropped off Cole and Dakota at their ranches and traveled on to Houston to meet Remi at her apartment.

In the meantime Ava and Remi were planning the wedding and Remi was desperately trying to pick out a wedding dress. Everything was rush-rush. Remi quit her job and moved out of her apartment. On Monday morning with the truck and car loaded down, they headed home to Rebel Ranch.

On Monday evening they got married in the little Catholic church in Horseshoe, Texas. When he saw Remi with Nathan on one side and Ava on the other, his heart swelled inside of him. He would never love anyone as much as he loved her. And when he saw the turquoise boots peeking out from the silk-and-lace dress he couldn't have loved her more than he did at that moment. She'd traded her heels for cowgirl boots.

Miss Bertie had gotten a perm for the wedding and Paxton hardly recognized her, but the biggest surprise was Ruger in a suit, walking Miss Bertie down the aisle. He had a feeling Ava had something to do with that. Ruger was here and he knew it made Remi happy that her brother had participated in the wedding. The reception was at Rebel Ranch and later that evening they got into his truck and drove to Port Aransas where they'd first met. They took long walks on the beach and warmed up in the Jacuzzi together. It was idyllic. It was just them and they didn't need anything else. They came home late Wednesday because it was Christmas week and they wanted to be home for the holiday.

They moved into the old homeplace, where Falcon and Leah had once lived. They had moved across the road into their new home and the place was vacant and available. It was perfect for what they needed. They would decide later if they wanted to build a house or whatever. It didn't matter to Paxton. He just wanted to be with Remi.

They had left Sadie at Miss Bertie's when they had gone on their honeymoon and she was still there. They planned to pick her up today.

Paxton crawled out of the bed and slipped into his underwear. Pulling on his jeans, he noticed Remi beneath the covers, her hair everywhere, the way he liked it—tousled. Leaning over, he gently moved her hair to kiss her cheek.

"Sleep in, beautiful lady."

She stirred and sat up. "What time is it?"

"Almost six." He sat on the bed to pull on his socks.

"Why are we up… Oh, you're going to help Elias this morning and I have an interview at the school for a job."

"Yep. And then I'll meet you back here at noon and we'll go over to your grandmother's, and Ruger and I are going to rebuild her corral as a Christmas gift."

"She'll love it."

"She'll love that it doesn't cost her a dime."

She wrapped her arms around his neck from behind and pressed her body against him. "I don't want to be away from you too long."

"Me, neither." He turned his head to kiss her. "I thought you would be tired this morning."

"I am. You kept me up all night."

"I'm not the one who was nibbling on my ear at two o'clock this morning."

She rested her head on his shoulder. "Are you complaining?"

"Never."

A knock sounded at the door. "I'll get it," Paxton said. "It's probably Elias ready to go to work."

As he opened the door, he was startled to see his mother. "Mom."

"Good morning, son." She held up a basket with a red gingham cloth over it. "I made breakfast muffins and I brought some for you and Remi."

He took the basket from her. "Thank you."

"Who is it?" Remi came into the room in nothing but a T-shirt. Paxton stepped aside so his mother could come into the house.

"Good morning, Remi. I brought breakfast."

"Oh, Miss Kate, that's so sweet of you."

"Have y'all settled into the house?"

Remi came to his side and he wrapped an arm around her waist. "I love this old log house," Remi replied. "It feels like home."

"I was planning on doing some upgrades," Paxton said.

"Whatever you want," his mother replied. And then

she touched his face and so many feelings ran through him. His mother had been through so much and he hated that he had caused her pain. Hopefully, that side of him was gone. "I'm so proud of the way you've changed this past year. You have grown into the young man your father knew you would be."

"Thank you, Mom."

She turned to Remi. "At first, I have to admit that I had doubts, but when I look at you I don't see Ezra. I just see your beautiful face and personality. You're the perfect mate for my son and I wish you two nothing but happiness." Remi and his mother hugged tightly. "Now I have to go and leave you two lovebirds alone."

As the door closed, Remi went into his arms. "I like your mother."

So did he. "Mmm."

Remi went into the kitchen to make coffee. "I'm going to take a shower and then we'll eat breakfast." She headed toward the bathroom and he went back into the bedroom to finish dressing. A phone buzzed and he saw it was Remi's on the dresser. He leaned over to see who it was. *Constance Baxter.* Who was that? Then he remembered. Remi's lawyer. Why was she calling? The only way to find out was to answer it.

"This is Paxton Rebel."

"Oh, I was trying to reach Remi Roberts."

"She's Remi Rebel now. We're married."

"Congratulations. I'm happy for you."

"Why are you calling, Ms. Baxter?"

"There's been a development in Annie's case and I thought Remi might like to know."

"What happened?" Inside he was screaming, *No,*

no, not now! They were happy. Remi didn't need to be hurt again.

"I would rather speak to Remi."

"She's taking a shower and I'd rather that you talked to me because I'm not having her upset like the last time."

"I need to move on this quickly, so please tell Remi that Mrs. Wallace has had a mental breakdown and has been institutionalized. Her husband has returned Annie to the state because he now has to care for his wife. Seems the woman was so worried about Annie's heart surgery that she watched her constantly and rarely slept or ate. The husband tried to talk to her but she wouldn't listen. Apparently the three miscarriages and then adopting Annie was too much for her. Finally, she just collapsed and she doesn't know who she is or where she is. The bottom line is, Mr. Rebel, the state now has to deal with Annie and find her a home. I thought Remi would want to know that."

Anger filled his lungs. "They made the wrong decision and now Annie is suffering for that."

There was a long pause on the line. "Yes, but if Remi wants Annie, we have to get started immediately. They're giving us a heads-up and that's a big plus sign. Please have her call me."

"Where's Annie now?"

"She's at Texas Children's being evaluated. She's fine, though."

"Hasn't the adoption gone through by now?"

"According to Ms. Connors, they've had a lot of problems with the Wallaces. They balked at home visits and failed to get paperwork in when they needed to.

They were getting ready to stop the adoption and remove Annie when Mr. Wallace called."

"Did they change her name?"

"Legally, no."

"I'll tell Remi and if she's interested she'll call you right back." Paxton laid the phone on the dresser. He didn't know how Remi was going to react. They hadn't talked any more about Annie. They put her out of their minds because they had to. Now Remi was secure in their love and...

Remi came into the bedroom with a towel wrapped around her body and rubbing her hair with another towel.

"Did I hear my phone?" she asked.

"Yeah." He sat on the bed and patted the spot beside him. "I have something to tell you."

She did as instructed and held the towel in her hand. "What is it? You look so serious."

"It's about Annie." And he told her what Ms. Baxter had said.

Her eyes opened wide. "Oh. Is Annie okay?"

Paxton nodded. "She's at Texas Children's being evaluated." He watched her face and saw nothing but sadness. "What do you want to do?"

She stared down at the towel in her hand. "I'm happy now. Really happy, and I can't go through another custody hearing. It hurt too much."

"You said Annie was your last chance and she was the child of your heart."

She raised her eyes to his, and he saw the tears about to break through. "Annie is all alone in that hospital at Christmastime."

"Do you want to change that?"

She stood up and grabbed her phone. "It makes me so angry at what that agency has done to Annie." She looked at her phone and then at him. "Are you ready to be a father?"

He smiled, and pulled out his phone. Holding it up, he said, "Look, I still have all the pictures you sent me of Annie. I tried to delete them, but couldn't. Now I know why. She was meant to be our little girl."

"Oh, Paxton." She threw her arms around his neck and they held on for a few minutes, savoring this moment of knowing they might get Annie back.

Remi made the call and he was in awe of what she was saying. "Ms. Baxter, they screwed up. Really bad, and this hurts Annie. Here's what I'm willing to do. No long adoption process interviewing couples who might be ideal parents for Annie. No waiting. I'm not going to be put through that pain again. My husband and I will come to Houston and pick up Annie and adopt her. The agency will have papers ready to sign. Annie doesn't need to spend Christmas in the hospital. You make that happen and we'll be there within two hours. They made a mistake and I'm giving them the chance to make it right. Make it happen, Ms. Baxter." She laid down the phone with a smile.

Paxton grabbed her. "Wow. What was her response?"

"She has to talk to the judge, and she will call me back within the hour. So now we wait."

Remi sat on the bed. "Annie's a year old now. I wonder if she will recognize me."

"When's her birthday?"

"It was December 12. My wreck was in October and…"

He took her hand and led her into the kitchen. "No sad thoughts. Let's eat breakfast while we wait."

Someone pounded on the door. Paxton groaned. "Elias. I forgot all about him with the Annie thing going on."

He swung open the door to find Elias and Jericho standing there. "I just wanted to let you know that Jericho offered to help me with the fence. Enjoy the honeymoon." He saluted and walked off. There was no one like Elias. He loved work and it reminded Paxton of his dad, who had been the same way.

Jericho nodded at him. "Don't worry. I got you covered. I mean, I've been eating peach cobbler all summer so I at least owe you something."

"Thanks, Rico." Miss Bertie had been sending peach cobblers and Rico would text him when one came to the bunkhouse. Paxton would tell him to just eat it.

The next hour was the longest of their lives. They ate breakfast and then finished dressing. Paxton called his mother to let her know what was going on and Remi called her grandmother and her parents. She canceled her interview. Paxton turned on the TV and quickly turned it off. Remi paced and Paxton watched her. She was hurting all over again and there was nothing he could do to stop it.

An hour later there was no phone call.

"Why isn't she calling?" Remi asked. "What if they decide to put Annie through the whole adoption process again?"

"Hey, where's all that confidence I heard earlier?"

"I just get so mad when I think of what's been done to Annie's life and now..."

He kissed her cheek. "She will call. Just stay calm."

But an hour and fifteen minutes later there was still

no phone call. Paxton's confidence was beginning to waver, too.

Remi threw up her hands. "I've had it." She reached for her phone on the table, and the moment she touched it, it buzzed. "It's Ms. Baxter." She picked up her phone and put it on speakerphone.

"I have you on speakerphone. What's their answer?" Remi came right to the point.

"I'm sorry it's taken me longer to call you back, but Judge Tomlin was busy and I had to wait to see her. But she agrees that Annie doesn't need to spend Christmas in the hospital. She's awarding temporary custody of Annie to you and your husband until all the paperwork is finished. There will be lots of paperwork. But it's a done deal. I will have papers ready to sign Friday morning for you to take her home, but in the meantime you're free to visit her anytime."

"Thanks, Ms. Baxter," Paxton said. "You've just made this the best Christmas ever."

"I'm just glad this has a happy ending. One more thing—they still have to do an interview with you guys and they have to come to your home to see where Annie will be living. And there will be more visits until the adoption is finalized. But you can handle that, right?"

"Right."

"I specifically asked that they make the interview and visit in mid-January to give you time to settle in. I don't foresee any problems."

"Thank you," Remi said, and placed her phone on the table. Then she jumped up and down with joy. "We're going to be parents and we just got married. I hope I'm ready for this. I hope you're ready for this."

He gathered her into his arms. "Oh, beautiful lady, I'm always ready."

ON FRIDAY AFTERNOON, they brought Annie home. Paxton had asked that everyone stay away until Annie was adjusted. Annie had certainly grown since they had seen her. She wasn't walking but she was pulling up on everything. And her hair was longer and was curling more. When she saw Remi the first time, she pulled up on the crib and held out her arms. At that moment Remi knew everything was going to be okay.

When they arrived home, they had a pleasant surprise. Phoenix and Jude had picked up Annie's crib and all her baby things from Remi's parents' house. They'd even painted the room white and pink and a beautiful Disney border graced the top of the walls. The white crib had Disney sheets and a blanket; there was also a changing table, diapers, toys and anything a baby would need, even a baby monitor. There was a note on the coffee table: *hope you like it. If you don't, you can change it.* It was signed, *The family.* Remi was overwhelmed they'd taken the time to do this. But they were her new family. The Rebel family always stood by each other, Gran had said, and she believed it.

Looking around the room, she saw all the love they had put into fixing it up. Remi wouldn't change a thing. She loved it.

She picked up her daughter, who was playing with a stuffed animal on the floor. "Look, this is your room."

Annie reached out her arms to Paxton, and he quickly took her. She watched them. Annie played with the pocket on his Western shirt and Paxton held her as if she was the most precious thing on earth. Her heart filled with love and happiness and she didn't think it was possible to be this happy or fulfilled.

She stroked Annie's hair, looking at her husband. "How does it feel, Daddy?"

Paxton smiled the biggest smile she'd ever seen. "Like heaven."

She knew what he meant. Their lives would change once again, but this time it would be for the better. They say that dreams don't come true, but Remi now believed in dreams, fairy tales and happy endings. And she saw everything she ever wanted in Paxton's eyes and in the eyes of her daughter.

ON CHRISTMAS EVE, Paxton, Remi and Annie went to his mother's to celebrate the holiday. The whole Rebel family and Jericho were there. Kids were running everywhere and Annie fit right in. She was enthralled with her new cousins. Martha Kate was nine months old and crawling. No one knew how that happened since Quincy and Grandpa never put her down.

The two girls hit it off instantly. Martha Kate would take off crawling and Annie would follow. Then Annie would stop and turn and go the other way and Martha Kate would chase after her. They would stop every now and then to kiss each other. Remi and Jenny were filming everything like crazy.

Annie had a big red bow in her hair to match the new dress they'd bought her. Martha Kate had a bow in her hair but she'd pulled it out a long time ago. Jenny had tried to put it back in, but Martha Kate kept pulling it out. Paxton thought that probably showed the temperaments of the two girls. His little angel was going to be easygoing while Martha Kate would break the rules all the way.

The adjustment phase with Annie was easy. She slept

through the night and when she woke up she would start playing. She cried very little and that worried them. But when they talked about it they were sure the nurses at the hospital had something to do with it. They didn't have the time to pamper her and she'd learned to be independent.

Sadie was her number one fan. She now slept in Annie's room and the moment she woke up Sadie would bark to alert them. He'd never known Labs were so good with kids.

The family had eaten a big supper and had opened gifts and now they were just sitting around talking. Zane, Jude's son, and Eden, Falcon's oldest child, had Christmas music cranked up high. Elias was doing the jitterbug with Eden, and everyone was watching. Even though Elias didn't drink around their mother, he was acting crazy tonight and Paxton wondered if he'd put something in the spicy apple cider their mother had made. But crazy was normal for Elias.

Their mother stood up and tapped her glass with a spoon. "Does anyone have news to share with the family?"

Phoenix popped up like a jack-in-the-box. "Rosie and I are pregnant!" he shouted and raised his arms. After that, there were kisses and hugs all around. Rosie wiped away tears. Paxton was happy for them and he wasn't envious. He had what he wanted—Remi—and it didn't matter if they had Annie or not. He loved her that much.

Jude stood up. "No hugs or kisses required, but Paige and I are expecting, too."

Elias grabbed Jude around the neck and kissed him. Everyone laughed.

Jenny stood up next. "I'd like everyone to know what

I've decided to do about Quincy's possessiveness of Martha Kate."

"I know. He won't let me hold her more than five minutes," Grandpa grumbled.

"That's about to change," Jenny added. "We're expecting our second child in August."

"Good heavens, y'all are populating like rabbits," Elias said.

"Elias." His mother looked at him, and Elias held his glass up for a toast.

"To all the new little rug rats!"

"Elias!"

Elias smiled stupidly. There was just no other way to put it.

"Merry Christmas, everyone." Their mother held up her glass as did everyone else.

Annie rubbed her eyes and Paxton knew she was getting sleepy. Suddenly, she turned on all fours and crawled directly to him, pulling on his jeans. He was surprised because she usually went to Remi. Lifting her into his arms, every fatherly instinct he had came to life and he couldn't love this little girl any more even if she was his biological child.

Remi patted Annie's back. "She loves her daddy."

"She's asleep. Maybe we should go home."

Remi hooked her arm through his and leaned against him. "She's fine, and Eden's about to make an announcement."

"Hey, everyone." Eden clapped her hands to get everyone's attention. "We're going to turn out the lights and sing 'Silent Night' with only the tree lights shining. Everybody ready?"

Zane flipped off the lights and everyone started to

sing. Grandpa's deep voice rose above the others. The tree lights sparkled on the nine-foot Douglas fir as happy voices filled the room.

"I love you," Remi whispered.

He kissed her lips. "Sweet lady, I'll spend a lifetime telling you how much I love you." Paxton looked toward the double French doors to the sky and could see a quarter moon hanging low like a big old smile. And he knew his dad was watching over the Rebel family. How else could they have gotten a miracle? They'd gotten Annie.

Now all they had to do was the living.

Paxton Rebel was a happy man.

* * * * *

There's only one bachelor brother left!
Read Elias's story in TEXAS REBELS: ELIAS,
coming December 2017, only from
Harlequin Western Romance!

Get 2 Free Books,

HARLEQUIN Western Romance

Plus 2 Free Gifts—
just for trying the Reader Service!

Jason Till is the type of cowboy Sloane Hartley wants to avoid. But she can't seem to stop thinking about him...

Read on for a sneak preview of
HER TEXAS RODEO COWBOY,
part of Trish Milburn's
BLUE FALLS, TEXAS *series!*

By the time her mom rang the bell signaling lunch was ready, Sloane had learned that Jason was from Idaho, he'd been competing as a professional since he was eighteen and he'd had six broken bones thanks to his career choice.

"Are you eating with us?" Phoebe asked as she slipped her little hand into Jason's.

He smiled down at her. "I don't think they planned for the extra mouth to feed."

Sloane huffed at that. "You've never met my mother and her penchant for making twice as much food as needed."

"Please," Phoebe said.

"Well, how can I say no to such a nice invitation?"

Phoebe gave him a huge smile and shot off toward the picnic area.

Jason chuckled. "Sweet kids."

"Yeah. And resilient."

He gave her a questioning look.

"They come from tough backgrounds. All of them have had to face more than they should at their age."

"That's sad."

"It is. They seem to like you, though."

"And that annoys you."

"I didn't say that."

"You didn't have to." He grinned at her as he grabbed a ham-and-cheese sandwich and a couple of her mom's homemade oatmeal cookies.

"Sorry. I just don't know you, and these kids' safety is my responsibility."

"So this has nothing to do with the fact your sister is trying to set us up?"

"Well, there goes my hope that it was obvious only to me."

"It's not a bad idea. I'm a decent guy."

"Perhaps you are, but you're also going to be long gone by tomorrow night."

He nodded. "Fair enough."

Well, that reaction was unexpected. She'd thought he might try to encourage her to live a little, have some harmless fun. She wasn't a fuddy-duddy, but she also wasn't hot on the idea of being with a guy who'd no doubt been with several women before her and would be with several afterward.

Of course, she often doubted a serious relationship was for her either. She'd seen at a young age what loving someone too much could do to a person. The one time she'd believed she might have a future with a guy, she'd been proved wrong in a way that still stung years later.

Don't miss HER TEXAS RODEO COWBOY
by Trish Milburn, available September 2017
wherever Harlequin® Western Romance
books and ebooks are sold.

www.Harlequin.com

EXCLUSIVE LIMITED TIME OFFER AT
www.HARLEQUIN.com

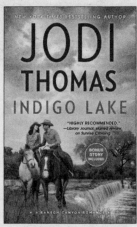

$7.99 U.S./$9.99 CAN.

$1.⁰⁰ OFF

New York Times Bestselling Author
JODI THOMAS
INDIGO LAKE

Two families long divided by an ancient feud. Can a powerful love finally unite them?

Available July 18, 2017.
Get your copy today!

Receive **$1.00 OFF** the purchase price of
INDIGO LAKE by Jodi Thomas
when you use the coupon code below on Harlequin.com.

INDIGO1

Offer valid from July 18, 2017, until August 31, 2017, on www.Harlequin.com.

Valid in the U.S.A. and Canada only. To redeem this offer, please add the print or ebook version of INDIGO LAKE by Jodi Thomas to your shopping cart and then enter the coupon code at checkout.

HQN™
www.HQNBooks.com

PHCOUPJT0817

Reward the book lover in you!

Earn points from all your Harlequin book purchases from wherever you shop.

Turn your points into *FREE BOOKS* of your choice
OR
EXCLUSIVE GIFTS from your favorite authors or series.

Join for FREE today at
www.HarlequinMyRewards.com.

Harlequin My Rewards is a free program (no fees) without any commitments or obligations.

MYR17

Looking for more satisfying love stories
with community and family at their core?

**Check out Harlequin® Special Edition
and Harlequin® Western Romance books!**

New books available every month!

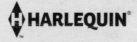